BULLY SQUAD
Jack Scoltock

All rights reserved. No part of this book may be utilised in any form or by any means, electronic or mechanical, including, photography, filming, recording, photocopying or by any information storage and retrieval system, or shall not by way of trade or otherwise be lent, resold, or otherwise circulated in any All rights reserved. No part of this book may be utilised in any form or by any means, electronic or form of binding or cover other than that in which it is published, without prior permission in writing from the publisher, Jack Scoltock. The moral rights of the author have been asserted.

From the author of many children's stories:

Including:
Davey's Siege (A Siege of Derry story)
Brothers
Going Back to Neverland
Patrick's Gift
Justine's Secret Challenge
Perry's Adventure
The Sand Clocker (Spanish Armada Stowaway)
Seek the Enchanted Antlers
Challenge of the Red Unicorn

BULLY SQUAD
Jack Scoltock

1

Jack's father stopped their small Fiat Panda car parallel to the water at the far end of the rough car park near the tufts of long grass that bordered the wide curving beach of Cardigan Bay. As they got out they looked up. The sky was blue and not a breeze rippled the calm water. It was going to be perfect. It was a perfect morning for snorkeling and one Jack would never forget for the rest of his life.

Smiling, father and son began to pull their masks, snorkels, weight-belts and wetsuits out of the boot and lay them carefully on the sandy grass. Shortly they were changing into their wetsuits.

Jack grinned when he saw his father, standing on one leg trying to pull on a fin. With a wild "Whoop!" he almost fell over.

Patrick and his son had often snorkeled in the clear waters of the Bay. Normally the beach would have been busy on such a beautiful summer's day, and it would be in an hour or so, when the first day-trippers would arrive.

"Time enough for us to have a good snorkel," said Jack's father that morning early, as they ate their breakfast.

Patrick O'Hara, who was an IT consultant, was a tall muscular man with a round, pleasant face. Jack was tall for a boy aged fourteen. He had blonde hair and freckles dotted his upturned nose.

"Try to be back before 1pm, Pat," said Jane, Jack's mother. "Remember we have the week's shopping to do this afternoon."

Jane was a beautiful red-haired woman, whose face and arms were covered in freckles, proof of that lovely summer.

"What if we get eaten by sharks?" said Patrick, winking at Jack. "You'll have to do the shopping on your own."

Jane smiled. "If you get eaten by sharks there will be all the more food for me and Daisy." She looked at her daughter who also had red hair.

"Mummy, why can't I go with them?" asked Daisy.

Jack gave a start. He didn't want Daisy coming. This was their time, his and his daddy's. He looked at his father who glanced at him and said, "Maybe next year, Daisy, when you're thirteen."

Jack raised his eyebrows in a teasing way to his sister.

Daisy glared at her older brother.

"But why can't I go? I can swim better than he can," she snapped.

It was true. She had often beaten her brother in swimming races at their local pool.

"You cannot," snapped Jack.

"I can, and you know it," retorted Daisy.

"You can't."

"Can."

"Can't."

"Ca…"

"Here, here you two," snapped their father. "That's enough."

"But Daddy," cried Daisy. "Why can't I come with you as well?"

Patrick looked at Jane then said, "Because…"

"Because what?" snapped Daisy, who was standing now with her fists clenched tightly, her knuckles white.

"Daisy love, sure I need you to help me do out the utility room this morning," said Jane quickly.

Daisy sighed. "Why can't Jack help you? He gets going everywhere. I get going nowhere." A tear pushed to the corner of her left eye. "You don't love me," she exclaimed, glaring at her father, as tears tumbled down her face.

"Ach don't love. Sure you know that's not true."

"It is!" shouted Daisy pushing away from the table and pointing at her brother. "You love him, but you don't love me!" Crying she ran to the sitting room door.

"Daisy!" called her father, when they all heard her run upstairs. Sighing

Patrick made to rise to his feet. "I'll go up to her."

"Ach leave her Pat. It'll only make her worse," said Jane. "She'll cool down after a while." She looked at the cooker. "That soup should be ready now."

In her room, Daisy wiped her wet eyes with the end of her blanket. She wanted to tell her parents that really the reason she was crying was because of the bullies. But she daren't. Megan had warned her that if she told anyone she would be sorry. The bullies had told Daisy they would get her out of school.

****

Now kitted up, Jack and his father spat into their masks and rubbed the spittle around the inside of the tempered glass. They were standing knee-deep in the water. They dipped their masks into the water and swirled them around a couple of times. Jack's father helped him fit his mask perfectly over his face, under the front of the hood of his wetsuit, making sure there was a good seal so as not to let any water flood in.

A minute later, after checking his son's weight-belt was fitted properly, Patrick led the way slowly out until he was waist deep and Jack was chest deep in the water.

Jack shivered at the initial coldness as the water soaked through his neoprene wetsuit to his body. It took a little over thirty seconds before he began to warm up, but soon he was snorkeling beside his father out of the gully and into the deeper water.

They finned easily for about twenty-five meters when Patrick turned suddenly and making strange gurgling noises through his snorkel pointed below.

Jack's eyes widened and his breathing increased when he saw a huge spotted fish just slipping into the thick seaweed about four meters below. Spluttering he panicked and treading water snapped his snorkel from his mouth. "Wha… what is it Daddy? It…it looks like a…a…" He was afraid to say the word.

"A spotted dogfish," said Patrick, easily treading water beside him.

"It…it looked like a shark," said Jack. He could feel his heart still pounding.

"Well it is a requiem fish- a member of the shark family." Patrick grinned at the look on his son's face.

"Ach but they're harmless, really. Come on, let's fin further on out."

They snorkeled on out into deeper water, back and forth pointing and watching several shoals of Pollack and other tiny fish swim for cover into the thick seaweed. White sea-urchins, their soft spines wafting in the light current dotted the seaweed. Once a huge crab scuttling sideways caught their attention and for several minutes they snorkeled below to get a better look at it.

Fifteen minutes later, Jack's father tapped him on the shoulder and pointed to some rocks on the left hand side of the bay indicating they were to snorkel to them.

When they were about twenty-meters from the rocks, a splash of light in the water to Jack's left drew his attention. Then they saw it. Father and son treaded water, as they watched the beautiful porpoise leap to the surface not far from them, its sleek body glistening in the sunlight. It bounded closer and closer until it was only a few meters from Jack and his father. Jack was too frightened to breathe as the porpoise floated on the surface and stared with one eye almost right into his face. Jack was afraid, yet at the same time he wasn't. Suddenly the porpoise leapt right out of the water and landed with a little splash beside him then disappeared below. They both looked under the water, watching as the creature shot to the bottom of the bay then slowly began to rise, its eyes fixed on them. Then all of a sudden it shot to the bottom again and was away. For the next two minutes they searched the bottom, but the porpoise had gone.

11

"Did…did you see it? Did you Daddy?" Jack exclaimed his face beaming.

"Yes," said Patrick. He smiled. "If you and I could swim like that it…" He scanned the surface of the water. "Well, it looks like it's gone. Come on, let's head back…Let's head…"

Head back, thought Jack, just when I'm beginning to enjoy himself. He studied his daddy as he adjusted the strap on his mask. Patrick looked very pale and was shaking his head from side to side. Instantly Jack knew something was wrong.

****

Three minutes later they were finning through the gully into the shallow water. As they lay in the water their masks and snorkels lying on the rocks beside them, Jack exclaimed, "It was a big one Daddy, wasn't it."

"The biggest I've ever seen up close."

"It was fast too."

"The fastest," muttered Patrick suddenly reaching to hold his stomach.

"Wait until we tell Mummy. She'll never believe us," said Jack slowly as he studied his father. He didn't seem to have heard him.

"Daddy…"

Patrick turned. "Jack, maybe we shouldn't say anything about the porpoise when Daisy's about. She'll only get upset again."

"But Daddy…"

"Come on," said his father rising from the water. "Let's get out of our wetsuits. That hot soup is waiting for us."

Shortly they were sitting on the grass in their wetsuit long-johns with their snorkeling gear lying all around them. Patrick had filled two plastic cups with the steaming vegetable soup and as they drank it they could feel the hot liquid quickly warming them.

Just then a car drove onto the car park. They watched for a while as the occupants, a family of five got out. One of the children had a kite and soon they were all running onto the beach.

Suddenly, movement out in the water caught Jack's attention. He pointed. Away out they could see several sea gulls plummeting to the water.

"There must be plenty of fish out there," said Patrick. "That must have been what drew the porpoise into the bay."

Jack scanned the horizon and across the bay to the far side. There was no sign of the porpoise.

A couple of minutes later, Jack's father poured some more soup into his cup. Then he did a strange thing, something that Jack would always remember. He reached for his mask and poured the rest of the soup into it. Jack laughed at what he thought was a joke. But he stopped laughing when he saw his father was staring stupidly at the mask.

"Daddy..." Jack could feel his heart beating. Something wasn't right with his daddy. He knew it.

Patrick turned. There was a strange vacant look on his face.

Jack nodded to the mask of soup he was holding. The soup was trickling over the silicone seal onto his father's legs.

Patrick stared down at it then threw the mask and its contents onto the grass. When he looked at Jack again his face was clouded in anger. "Come on, let's wash the sand out of our gear and get home. Your mother will be waiting for us."

All the way home, Jack's father hardly spoke to him.

****

Around 10pm that evening Jack slipped downstairs for a glass of milk. The mouthful or two of sea water he had swallowed whilst snorkeling had made him thirsty. As he came into the kitchen he could hear his mother and father talking.

"Look Patrick, you'll just have to go to the doctor. It's stupid to wait any longer."

"Ach, Jane, it's because I'm tired. You know I've been working hard on our new corporate website this past month. It's nothing…really."

"Patrick, it's not nothing. Whatever is wrong with you, it's getting worse. Please, just make an appointment with Doctor Stone. Do it for me, at least…"

Jack frowned. Something *is* wrong with my daddy, he thought. Quietly he filled his tumbler with milk, took a quick gulp then hurried into the sitting room.

"Ah don't worry love…" Patrick began again.

"What's wrong?" asked Jack searching his parent's faces.

"Wrong? What do you mean, son?" asked Patrick.

"I overheard Mummy saying you should see a doctor. What for?"

Jane glanced at Patrick.

"It's nothing for you to worry about, Jack." Patrick smiled. "I was telling your mother about the porpoise."

"Yes," said Jane. "I hear it came right up to you."

Jack smiled. "You should have seen it jump. It floated right up beside me and stared at me with its big eye…fantastic."

****

Later in bed, Jack thought about his daddy. Something is definitely wrong with him. Is he ill? He thought now about how he had got so carried away with telling his mother about the porpoise, he had forgotten to find out. As he drifted to sleep, he thought, I'll ask daddy about it in the morning.

2

When Jack came down to breakfast his father had already gone to work and Daisy was eating her breakfast cereal. As his mother filled his bowl with cornflakes he remembered.

"Mummy, why did you want Daddy to go to the doctors?"

Daisy, who had a huge spoonful of cornflakes halfway to her mouth, stopped and slowly lowered her spoon to the cereal bowl, "What's wrong with Daddy?" she asked.

"No…nothing," answered Jane quickly and turned to the sink. "He's just been a bit tired that's all. He's been working hard. He's promised to go to the doctors for a tonic."

"A tonic?" exclaimed Daisy, remembering when her grandfather, who had been ill for some time, had to take the foul tasting liquid. He had given her a taste and laughed when she had made a face. Her grandfather had passed away two months later. Daisy was only seven years old then. She had never forgotten it.

"Yes," said Jane glancing at the kitchen clock. "Now you two hurry up. You'll be late for school."

Daisy looked at Jack. She was wondering how he knew about her daddy being ill. Suddenly she grew angry, rose from the table and hurried from the kitchen. They never tell me anything, she thought, as she hurried upstairs to get her school blazer and books. Then her stomach heaved as she remembered about the bullies and with a cry she dived towards the toilet.

****

A few minutes later Jane watched as Daisy and Jack headed down the road to school together. With a heavy sigh she returned to the kitchen to tidy up and do the dishes. As she washed Jack's cereal bowl she stared out into their big back garden at the beautiful patio Patrick had built two summers ago, when he had been well. She remembered how she had helped him lift and lay the heavy flagstones. They had worked from a plan she had drawn… and all of a sudden she burst into tears.

****

"I think her hair's even redder than it was on Friday!"

Daisy froze, as Megan's hateful tinny voice came from behind her.

"How's Daisy, the red headed pube," giggled Megan's best friend, Danni Watson shoving Daisy hard in the small of her back. Danni was a black haired girl with a bright bow tied around the top of her shock of wild hair.

Suddenly uttering a swear word, a third girl with a pony tail, grabbed Daisy by the hair and forced the smaller girl against the playground wall. Several other girls nearby, pretending not to notice, hurried to the far side of the playground as the three bullies towered over Daisy.

"Have you brought the money, ginger snap?" hissed the third girl, who was called Elizabeth Downey, squeezing the front of Daisy's dress tightly in her fist holding her trapped against the wall.

"I…I couldn't get any," Daisy gasped. Her legs felt so weak she thought they wouldn't hold her up.

Suddenly Megan pushed Elizabeth aside and banged Daisy's head hard, against the wall then held her with both hands gripping the lapels of her blazer. Dazed, Daisy heard Megan Heaney, the leader of the bullies, hiss into her face, "We told you to bring the money today." Megan's nose ring was about a centimeter from Daisy's left eye.

As the bully spat into Daisy's face, she could see the stud in her tongue. The girls pushed Daisy harder against the wall, Elizabeth and Danni looked around to make sure none of the teachers were about.

"Owww," cried Daisy. "Please...I'll...I'll bring it tomorrow."

Megan glanced at her cronies then grabbed Daisy by her left ear and squeezed it so hard she forced the smaller girl almost to the ground.

"You promise," she grunted, squeezing harder.

"Owww, yes...yes. I...I promise, I promise," cried Daisy.

"You know what we'll do to you if you don't, don't you?" hissed Megan.

"Yes. I promise," cried Daisy.

Megan released her, but suddenly Danni pushed her aside and with a cry punched Daisy hard in the stomach. Gasping for breath, Daisy sank to the ground. As she did Megan snarled, "I think two pounds isn't enough." She grinned at her cronies. "Better make it three."

Daisy's tear-filled eyes widened. "T...three," she gasped. "But..."

"Yes," snarled Megan, grabbing Daisy by the hair and banging her head against the wall again. "You were told to bring two pounds today. You didn't. Next time we tell you to do something, do it. If you don't bring the three quid to school tomorrow you won't like what we'll do to you?"

Daisy frowned. Her head was throbbing and she felt sick. Tears were running down her face.

"You'll find out tomorrow if you don't bring the money," snapped Elizabeth. Suddenly with a curse she slapped Daisy hard on the side of her face.

"Come on," said Megan. "Let's get to the canteen. I'm hungry."

Sniffing back tears, Daisy watched the three bullies laughing as they walked to the entrance to the canteen. Three pounds, she thought. Where am I going to get three pounds? Suddenly she had to go to the toilet. Seconds later she was racing for the girls' toilets at the far side of the playground.

****

Later as she sat in class trying hard to concentrate on her English composition, she thought about the bullies. They were in Jack's class and they had begun to bully her three weeks ago. She had wanted to tell Jack and her parents, but the bullies had warned her. They had threatened that if she told anyone, especially the teachers; they would never stop bullying her. They told Daisy they could always get her outside of school.

What am I going to do? thought Daisy.

****

Around the same time, Patrick was sitting in Doctor Stone's office. After he had explained his symptoms, the doctor checked his heartbeat and blood pressure.

"Patrick I would like you to have a brain scan."

"What?" exclaimed Patrick studying the doctor, "a brain scan?" He frowned. "You think there's something wrong with my brain? It's that serious?"

"These lapses you've had- there has to be something causing them. I'd need to get further checks done before I can make a diagnosis." Stone bent to scribble something on a yellow piece of paper. "If you could hand this to the receptionist she'll make an appointment for you. I'd like to have the results back as soon as possible."

Patrick could feel his heart pounding like a hammer on a drum as he asked, "Doctor, what do you think is wrong with me?"

Doctor Stone looked through the window at the car-park. "I...I need to be sure Patrick. Let's wait for the results of the scan test eh."

****

That evening at home, just before supper, Jack noticed how quiet his father and mother were.

Daisy was up in her room doing her homework. When she was finished she thought about the bullies. Where am I going to get three pounds for tomorrow? Oh what am I going to do? She thought. Daisy had already borrowed her allowance for the week from her mummy and she knew she wouldn't get any more. Her mother was a stickler about their allowance. Daisy's stomach churned with fear as she thought about the beating she would get if she didn't bring the money.

"Daisy," called her mother. "Supper's ready."

With a sigh Daisy rose from her bed and hurried out onto the landing. As she was about to pass her parent's room she saw her mother's handbag lying on the bed near the bedside table. She stopped, her heart beat speeding up. She could hardly breathe as she thought about what she was going to do. Walking to the top of the stairs she listened, then, when she was sure no one was coming up, she dashed into her mother's room and quickly opened the handbag. There were two five-pound notes, a one pound coin and two fifty pence pieces and small change in her mother's purse. Silently, and with her heart pounding so hard she thought it would burst through her chest, she took one of the five-pound notes from the purse and slipped it into her pocket, closed her mother's bag and hurried to her room.

"Daisy, did you hear me?" shouted her mother.

"Coming Mummy!" shouted Daisy, slipping the money into her school blazer pocket. Then with her heart still pounding she hurried downstairs.

****

That night as she lay unable to sleep, she thought about what she had done. I've stolen, and from mummy too, she thought. "But…but I had to," she sniffed, as tears filled her eyes. "I had to."

It was a long time before she fell asleep and when she did she had a nightmare about Jack chasing her and shouting, "You took Mummy's money!"

3

That morning in the playground at break-time, the three bullies cornered her. "Well," snapped Megan. "Have you brought it?"

"Ye…yes," muttered Daisy, pulling the squashed five-pound note from her pocket.

"Give it to me," snapped Megan. She was about to reach for it when Danni grabbed it from Daisy's hand and laughing ran away. Megan glared after her then suddenly angry she punched Daisy in the face throwing the little girl back against the wall. "Next time I ask you to give *me* the money you'll do as you're told." Then looking across the playground at Danni she ran towards her.

"But you only wanted three pounds," shouted Daisy. "You only wanted three…" And suddenly she began to cry.

****

At eleven O'clock that morning, Miss Curtis, the Head Teacher came into the classroom. With her was a brown-haired, heavy-set girl, whose face was as pale as new paper. The big girl stood awkwardly to one side of the door as Miss Curtis hurried to Mr. Thompson the class teacher. As she whispered something to him, Tommy Moran, Jack's best pal, whispered, "Who's the elephant?" He nodded to the girl. Tommy was a slim boy with his black hair streaked with blonde.

Jack grinned as he studied the new girl who looked even more uncomfortable when the Head left and Mr. Thompson turned to the class.

"Class," he said smiling at the girl. "I'd like to introduce a new pupil. Her name is, Nora Hannigan. Nora, if you would take a seat beside Catherine there." He pointed to the nearest seat where Catherine Carlin, a skinny girl with a pock-marked face, sat.

Several girls, the three bullies, Jack and Tommy giggled when they saw Nora trying to squeeze into the narrow seat. The teacher glared down the room then waited until Nora was comfortable before saying, "Right class let's give Nora a great big welcome." He began to clap and soon the classroom echoed to the sound of everyone clapping.

****

In the canteen at dinnertime, Nora sat with Catherine and a girl called Maudie McNutt. Maudie was a pleasant looking girl with bright big blue eyes, eyes that wouldn't have looked out of place on a Barbie Doll.

"Where are you from?" asked Catherine, trying to get a conversation out of the quiet girl, who was picking with her fork at one of the school canteen's hamburgers.

"I've been living in Japan for the past two years," replied Nora glancing over at Jack, Tommy, and two other boys who were grinning and giggling and nodding over at the girls. "Mummy died and Daddy brought us here to live with my grandparents. They…" Nora glanced over at the boys. One of them was pointing at her and giggling.

Catherine turned, her eyes narrowing when she saw Jack and the others. "Ah Nora don't mind them. They're a bunch of ignoramus's, especially that Tommy Moran. He called me pimply bake, the other day and laughed. That Jack O'Hara's no better. He laughed too. It's my medicine that causes me to have bad skin. That's what the doctor says. I have to take it though. It's supposed to help my asthma." She glared across at the boys when there was another eruption of laughter from them.

****

In the playground that dinnertime, Daisy tried to stay out of the way of the bullies, but they cornered her near the bike shed.

"We want another two pounds tomorrow," hissed Megan glancing around to make sure they weren't being observed. It was just then that Nora, Catherine and Maudie came walking past. Nora stopped and studied the bullies and Daisy.

"Something bothering you, Fatty?" snapped Elizabeth.

Catherine tried to pull her on. "Come on, Nora. Come on," she repeated.

Nora hesitated. She glanced at Catherine and gave in to her new friend's persistent tugging on her sleeve. Before walking away she studied Daisy. She could see the little girl was frightened.

"Keep a wide berth of those three," whispered Catherine looking back. The three bullies were glaring after them. "They take E's and they're very violent. Last year they beat up one of the P6 girls. They hurt her really bad too. Everyone knew who did it, but no one had the guts to tell the Head."

"Who are they?" asked Nora looking across the playground at Jack, Tommy and the other boys. One of them pointed at her and they all laughed.

"Who, the girls?" asked Catherine. "Elizabeth Downey, Megan Heaney and Danni Minogue."

"Danni Minogue?" exclaimed Nora smiling.

Catherine laughed and so did Maudie, "Danni Watson, but that's what we call her."

Just then the school bell rang and everyone hurried into class.

****

That evening before supper, Jane called the children into the sitting room. Jack glanced at Daisy before following her into the room. Whenever they were summoned to the sitting room it was usually a sign that something important was to be discussed.

Jane glanced at Patrick then said quietly, "Children we have something to tell you."

Oh God, thought Jack. *They're getting a divorce.*

"Your Daddy's ill," said Jane. She was hardly able to get the word out. Ill seemed too timid a word to describe what was wrong with her husband.

Jack gasped and studied his father who sat with a stunned look on his face.

"Ill? What do you mean?"

"Your father is in the early stages of Alzheimer's Disease," said Jane, her mouth suddenly dry.

"What?" exclaimed Daisy. "What's Alz…Alz…?"

"Alzheimer's Disease," said her father rising and going to them. He looked down at the children. "It usually happens when someone is older, a lot older. It's unusual for anyone as young as me, in their early forties to have the symptoms." He studied the childrens' worried pale faces. "Look, I'll be OK, for years yet, hopefully. The doctor has given me some medicine. It will help slow down the disease."

"How…how will the disease affect you Daddy?" asked Jack. He could feel the stinging tears in his eyes. His daddy was ill, seriously ill and he knew there was nothing he could do to help him.

Patrick glanced at Jane. "He'll start to…to forget things," said Jane looking at Patrick.

"Forget things?" exclaimed Jack, remembering the day his father had poured the soup into his mask. It must have been starting then, he thought.

"Yes," answered Jane. "Little things…at first."

"Will he forget about us?" asked Daisy, tears welling up.

"Daisy you know I'd never forget about you," exclaimed her father, almost in tears himself. "Any of you."

His two children studied him. What can I say? He thought. How can I tell them my memory will get worse? How can I tell them I'll even forget how to tie my shoe laces? How can I tell them I might get violent? How can I tell them, I *will* forget who they are?

"Look, we'll be OK," he added glancing at Jane. He knew it would be harder on her. "You'll see. So stop worrying." He smiled. "Look, what say I go and get fish and chips for the lot of us? Anyone want to come with me?"

The chorused, "Me!" from his children eased the tension.

Looking through the window Jane saw her children at the passenger door arguing with each other who would sit in the front seat with their father.

When the car drove out of the drive, with Jack in the front seat, she began to cry. Why us, she thought, stumbling out to the kitchen to set the table. Why did it have to be Patrick?

When Patrick and the children returned, the family ate their meal in silence. Each was lost in their own thoughts, each afraid to broach the subject of Patrick's illness.

Jack was thinking, was this the end to their snorkeling days. Would his daddy be too ill to take him snorkeling in the Bay?

Daisy was thinking about the bullies. Perhaps if I told them my daddy is ill they'll leave me alone?

****

Next morning in the playground, Daisy tried to hide from the bullies by keeping close to a group of girls from the fifth grade. But just when she thought the bullies would leave her alone, Megan slipped behind, grabbed her by the arm, hissing into her ear, "Over to the far side, bitch." She forced the smaller girl across the playground to the toilet wall.

"Did you bring the money?" snapped Danni, glancing around to make sure no one could observe what they were up to.

"I…I could only get a pound," whispered Daisy, her stomach heaving. "I'm sorry. I…" Suddenly Megan slapped her hard across the face. The blow staggered the smaller girl throwing her back against the wall. Immediately the two bigger girls grabbed her by the arms and held her hard against the rough plastered wall. Glancing around to make sure no one noticed what they were up to Elizabeth pushed her face right up against the frightened girl's tearful one. "We said two pounds, bitch." She looked at the other two. "Didn't we say two pounds?"

"We said two pounds," hissed Danni forcing her elbow against Daisy's arm squeezing the muscle against the wall.

"Owww," gasped Daisy. "But I gave you five pounds yesterday…"

Suddenly Megan released her arm and slapped her again. "Where's the money?" she snapped.

Crying Daisy pulled the coin from her coat pocket and was just about to hand it to her when Danni snapped it from her hand. It was then she remembered Megan's threat. Megan snarled when Elizabeth and Danni laughing walked away.

"What did I tell you," she hissed grabbing Daisy by the throat. "Now tomorrow I want you to bring *me* five pounds."

"Five…but," began Daisy. Suddenly Megan punched her in the stomach and as Daisy, trying hard to catch her breath, bent over, she hissed, "I said five pounds and if you don't give it to *me*, God will you be sorry."

"My Daddy's ill," cried Daisy. "Please…leave me alone."

Megan glared at the crying girl. "If you don't bring me five pounds tomorrow, you'll be the one that's ill." Then she turned and hurried after the other bullies.

"Look there's fatty," whispered Jack pointing, as Nora came walking over with Catherine and Maudie.

"Watch this," whispered Tommy quickly folding his magazine. Then just as the girls were passing Tommy hit Nora a hard slap on the behind with his magazine.

Nora gave a short surprised skip then with an angry bellow she turned to see Jack, Tommy and several other boys laughing at her. The big girl glared at them for several seconds then turned and walked on with her new friends to the sound of the boys yelling, "Big fat elephant, Nora Hannigan!"

Nora was still trembling, when the girls walked through the door into class.

Just behind her, with her back slouched, came Daisy. How am I going to get five pounds? She thought. I can't. Oh God what am I going to do?

4

Late that night Daisy slipped downstairs. She could hear her mother and father talking in the sitting room. She heard her mother say the word, "Alzheimer's," a word she would grow to hate.

Daisy knew her mother's bag and purse were in the kitchen. I have to get the money, she thought. I have to. Listening to make sure her parents were still in the sitting room, she slipped to the table and opened her mother's leather bag. With her heart pounding, she reached inside the bag and pulled out her mother's purse. Quickly she opened it. Tucked into the side pocket of the purse were two five-pound notes. With her heart still pounding Daisy slipped one out and shoved the crumpled note into the pocket of her pajama top. She was just in time to replace her mother's purse when the door opened and Jack appeared.

"What are you doing?" he asked.

"D...doing? I...I couldn't sleep," whispered Daisy, trying her best to calm her pounding heart. *Did Jack see?*

"Neither could I," said Jack going to the fridge and taking out a carton of milk. "I'm worried about Daddy." He studied his sister's face. She looked paler than usual. "You OK? What happened to your face?"

"My face?"

"That bruise," said Jack pointing.

"Oh that, I banged it in the playground the day before yesterday," lied Daisy, anxious now to get back to her bedroom.

"Who's there?"

It was their mother. She appeared at the kitchen door. "You two should be in bed," she said smiling. She turned. Patrick was behind her.

"Not able to sleep, eh?" he said smiling. "Don't tell me I'm going to have to read you a story?"

Jack smiled. This was more like his old daddy. It had been a long time since he had read them a story. Then he said, "Daddy why *don't* you read us one? I would like that, what about you Daisy?"

Daisy, who was still anxious to get back to her bedroom looked at her mother, she didn't want her to see the five-pound note in her pajama pocket. The top had shallow pockets and Daisy knew if she bent over the money might fall out. She gulped. If my mummy and daddy find out what I've done I'll be for it. Suddenly she trembled.

"Daisy what's wrong?" asked Jane noticing. "Are you cold? Come on, let's get you back to bed, both of you," she added looking at Jack.

"What about that story Daddy?" asked Jack grinning.

"You mean it? You really want me to read you a story," asked Patrick.

"Yes," said Jack turning to Daisy. "What about you Daisy?"

"What?" snapped Daisy, growing suddenly angry.

"Daddy, reading us a story?"

"It will have to be a short one mind," said Jane.

"Why don't I read one from Daisy's library?" said Patrick. "What do you think Daisy?" he asked.

Daisy shrugged. "Whatever," she said trying hard not to show enthusiasm for it.

"Good, come on then, upstairs the two of you," said Jane.

Shortly they were in Daisy's room and Patrick was looking along her shelves of books. He slipped one out. "Have you read this one, Daisy?" he asked.

Daisy, by now was in her bed with her blanket held up tight around her neck.

"What's it called?" she asked.

"Inkheart, by Cornelia Funke," replied Patrick reading the blurb on the back of the book.

"No," said Daisy.

"I hope it's not one of those girly books," moaned Jack who was sitting on the wickerwork bedside chair near the small dressing table.

"It's about a girl," said Patrick, reading the blurb on the back cover. "And her father who repairs old books, it's about magic I think. You both liked stories with magic in them when you were younger." He smiled. "Shall I begin?"

"OK," said Jack not too enthusiastically.

Jane watched from the bedroom door as her husband began to read then she turned and hurried downstairs. He seems OK, she thought, but she knew he wouldn't be for long. She had noticed his memory lapses were growing more frequent and she wondered did her children notice. She remembered the other night as they sat watching television. She had brought them both a cup of coffee and a digestive biscuit. Patrick had stared at the biscuit sitting on the edge of his cup for over a minute. His frown deepening he looked at Jane and said, "What's that?"

"What?" asked Jane.

"That," snapped Patrick, suddenly growing angry as he reached for the biscuit tipping the coffee out of the cup onto the carpet. Of course he had apologized later, but the incident was just a rehearsal for what was to come, and Jane knew it.

Walking into the kitchen she took out her purse. She stared at the one five-pound note. Oh God, she thought. One of my children is a thief.

****

That night Daisy couldn't sleep. She had stolen money from her mother again. She knew, she just knew she would be found out. What then? She thought. If Jack found out he would be angry. Tears found their way to her eyes as she thought about her mother. Mummy has enough to worry about without finding out I'm a thief.

It seemed forever before it was time to rise for school.

5

That morning as she walked through the school gate with Jack, Daisy saw the bullies standing just inside.

Danni pointed at her and raised a closed fist.

Nearby was, Nora, Catherine and Maudie.

As Jack and Daisy came in, Tommy hurried to them and as they passed Nora and the other girls, Tommy whispered something to Jack and they both laughed. Daisy heard the word, "Fat."

Daisy looked at Nora. The big teenager's face was blazing as she glanced at Daisy. It was obvious the she was angry.

"What did you say?" whispered Daisy looking after Nora as she hurried on into school.

"I said," giggled Tommy, "Look, there goes Nora the big fat Dumbo."

"That's wasn't very nice," snapped Daisy.

"Wise up, Daisy," said Jack. "Sure it's only a bit of craic."

"Is it? I'm sure if you were…were…"

"Fat, like an elephant," exclaimed Jack, laughing aloud.

Tommy began to laugh too.

"You wouldn't like people saying things like that about you," snapped Daisy. She was angry with her brother. How could he laugh at something like that, but then, she thought, Jack always was perfect, he always got his own way. He was spoiled…spoiled rotten.

"Ach Daisy," said Tommy. "Big Nora doesn't mind. I'm sure she's used to it by now."

"Would you get used to it, if someone called you a horrible name all the time," snapped Daisy. "Like…like Tommy, the big skinny Giraffe."

"Daisy," hissed Jack looking at his friend who appeared angry.

"Well would you?" said Daisy. "No I bet you wouldn't. So why don't both of you, grow up!" With an angry snort she hurried on into school.

****

At dinner-time in the playground, Daisy tried to stay away from the bullies. She stood near Nora and her friends trying to pluck up the courage to apologize to the big girl for the way her brother had behaved. At the same time she was keeping an eye out for the bullies. Then just as she was about to walk over to Nora, Danni grabbed her from behind. "This way," the bully hissed. "You'd better have brought the money with you."

"Let…let me go!" shouted Daisy trying to pull away. But the bigger girl was too strong.

Frowning Nora saw what was happening and watched as Daisy was forced to the far side of the playground where the other two bullies waited.

"Well did you bring the money?" snarled Megan, pulling Daisy roughly away from Danni and throwing her back against the playground wall.

"Please…" cried Daisy. "I can't get any more. My Daddy's very ill. This is the last. I can't get any more money…" She pulled the five-pound note from her pocket.

With a snarl Megan tore it from her hand and pushed her back hard against the wall.

As Danni and Elizabeth held the crying girl, Megan stuffed the money in her pocket then turned to Daisy. She studied her. Daisy, with tears running down her face silently pleaded to be left alone.

"My Daddy's ill," cried Daisy.

The little girl's fear made Megan angry and all of a sudden she remembered her own father, a violent, brutal man whom she had wished many times would die. Suddenly she slapped Daisy with all her strength.

Even Danni and Elizabeth were shocked by how hard she had hit Daisy and released her.

Daisy slid to the ground and lay there.

"Now you've done it, you stupid bitch!" hissed Elizabeth. "Come on."

From across the playground Nora watched as the three bullies ran towards the school door. She stared at the figure of the little girl lying on the ground. Without a word to Maudie and Catherine she hurried across the playground.

When she reached Daisy she was sitting up. A red bruise and blood on the side of her mouth showed where Megan had hit her.

"Are you all right?" asked Nora, just as Catherine and Maudie ran up to them.

"What happened?" asked Maudie studying Daisy.

Daisy stared at them. She couldn't tell. "I…I fell," she whispered. She tried to rise and pull away from the big girl, but Nora held her firmly.

"Fell?" exclaimed Catherine looking across the playground at Megan and the others.

"It's OK," said Nora quietly. "Are you OK?"

"Ye...yes," said Daisy looking at the other two girls.

Nora turned to them. "Catherine, Maudie, would you leave us. I'll catch up with you later."

Catherine frowned. "It was Danni Minogue and that Megan one, wasn't it?" she said angrily.

"Catherine, it's OK. I'll handle this. You and Maudie head on into school. I'll see to..." she turned. "What's your name?"

"Daisy, Daisy O'Hara."

"O'Hara," exclaimed Nora. "Are you anything to Jack O'Hara?"

"He...he's my brother," said Daisy in a small voice as she looked at the other girls.

Nora frowned, but said quickly, "Catherine, you and Maudie head on in. I'll see to Daisy."

Catherine looked at Maudie. She shrugged her shoulders and the two girls walked away.

"See you inside!" shouted Catherine.

"Here, Daisy," said Nora. "Grab my arm. I'll help you to your feet."

As she was helped to her feet Daisy grimaced and gasped with pain.

"Does it hurt?" asked Nora.

"Just my arms," said Daisy, wondering why the big girl was helping her. She looked around. There was no sign of the bullies and almost everyone had gone into class. She studied Nora. "I'm...I'm sorry for the way my brother behaves towards you," she said quietly.

Nora smiled. "It doesn't matter. I've been insulted by the best and in several languages too."

"What?"

"In Japan, where I lived, I was bullied at school, just like you. Daisy you have to tell someone- your parents. It's the only way to get them to stop."

"I…I can't. My Daddy's ill. Mummy has enough to worry about. I…I can't."

"I told my Daddy. My Mummy was ill too. The bullying stopped after a while," said Nora.

By then they were walking towards the school door. Just before they went inside Nora said, "Daisy, if you like, you can stand with us at break time. I don't think the bullies would come near you if you were with us." She frowned. "Those three are in your brother's class, aren't they? Haven't you told him?"

"Who? Jack?" Daisy shook her head. "What could he do? He's only interested in being popular. He wouldn't do anything," she said bitterly.

"He might, if you tell him what the bullies did to you. Daisy, they'll hurt you worse, eventually. They'll keep on and on…what do they want?"

"Money," whispered Daisy, a tear finding its way to er left eye. "I…I…" She stopped. She was going to tell Nora that she stole money from her mother to give to the bullies, but she didn't. "Thank you…Nora. Are…are you sure it's OK to stand with you at break time?"

"Of course," said Nora smiling. "We'll beat the bullies, you'll see." Nora looked up the corridor. "We'd better hurry, lessons have started."

As they ran up the corridor Daisy felt a little happier. Nora will protect me, she thought, Nora and the other bigger girls.

6

That evening at tea, Daisy lied about the bruise on her face saying she had walked into the heavy canteen door at school. She noticed that her brother was looking at her in an odd way.

Later, everyone went into the sitting room to watch Television.

As they watched their favorite soap, Jack studied his mother. All through tea he had noticed how quiet she was. He had put it down to worrying about his father, but she kept glancing at him. He knew something was bothering her. He glanced over now at his daddy. He was dozing on the big armchair. He had been sleeping a lot.

"It's the pills," his mother had explained earlier. "They make your Daddy sleepy."

When the soap serial was over, Jane held her finger to her lips telling them to be quiet then nodded for them to follow her,

Puzzled they hurried out to the kitchen and sat down at the table.

"What's wrong, Mummy?" asked Daisy.

Her mother frowned then gulped as she said, "Yesterday evening, one of you two took a five-pound note from my purse."

At the start of their protests Jane held up her hand. "Look I know it was one of you. I had missed the five-pound note that was taken the day before, so I put two five-pound notes together in the small pocket of my purse. All I want to know is, which of you took it, *stole* it?" she added, glaring at her children.

"It wasn't me," exclaimed Jack, unable to keep his face from going red. He looked at Daisy. "It must have been her."

"Me? Wise up," exclaimed Daisy, trying to keep calm. "What would I want five pounds for?

"All I know is, it wasn't me," snapped Jack. "So it must have been you."

"Well it wasn't," said Daisy, hoping her mother couldn't hear her heart pounding with fear. She felt as if she would vomit.

Jane studied her children. She was disappointed with them, disappointed and angry, and hurt, hurt that one of her children would steal from her. Suddenly she felt like crying.

"Haven't I enough problems without one of you stealing from me? She sniffed. "Well, whoever it is, are you going to own up?"

"Mummy, it wasn't me," cried Daisy realizing how very upset her mother was. But she couldn't tell her.

"And it wasn't me," said Jack. He glared at his sister. "Daisy, I know it was you. I know, because it wasn't me."

"I didn't steal the money, Mummy," cried Daisy. "You have to believe me…I…"

"You're lying!" shouted Jack.

Just then his father appeared at the door.

"What's all the shouting about?" asked Patrick looking at them.

"It's…it's nothing for you to be worrying about, Patrick," said Jane going to him. "Come on, it's time for your pills." She glanced back at Daisy and Jack before guiding Patrick out of the kitchen.

As Jack heard them going upstairs he rounded on Daisy. "Why did you steal from Mummy?" he said. "Look Daisy you can tell me. We'll sort this out together." He studied his sister.

"But it wasn't me," said Daisy unconvincingly.

"I know it was you, because it wasn't me," snapped Jack. "What did you need the money for that was so important you had to steal it?" He frowned. "Are you doing E's? Is that it? It is, isn't it? I've seen you with Danni and Megan. Daisy you know those two are troublemakers. Look, if it's drugs, I'll stand by you. Mummy will understand. We'll get it sorted."

"It…it's not drugs…" stammered Daisy. "It's…" But she knew she couldn't tell him. The bullies said they would get her if she told, and how could her brother help anyway. "Look," she cried, "Just leave me alone. Leave…me…alone!" With that she ran up the stairs and into her room and locked the door.

All of a sudden she was lying on her bed crying softly in case her mother would hear her.

****

In the kitchen Jack sat down. He tried to think. Surely Daisy wouldn't be doing drugs, not at her age, but he had heard of some other children who had been doing drugs, drinking alcohol, one of them had died. "Daisy wouldn't steal," he said aloud. "Not from Mummy, not now, not when…Daddy…is so…" and suddenly he felt tearful. He looked at the back door then slipped outside into the garden. It was raining lightly, but he didn't care. His whole family was falling apart. First his daddy, now Daisy.

****

That night Jane stopped in at each of her children's bedrooms.

"Mummy," said Jack. "It wasn't me, and if it wasn't me, it was Daisy. It was. Mummy I've never lied to you, never."

Jane studied her son's face. Jack was a little spoiled, but he was a good boy. She believed him.

"We'll discuss this later," she said tucking in the side of Jack's blanket. "Maybe…maybe I was mistaken…" she added then smiling she left the room.

Slipping into Daisy's room she saw that she was sleeping. I'll not disturb her tonight, she thought. But I must find out why she needed the money, why she couldn't ask me for it, why she had to steal it.

Daisy listened until she heard the creaky step at the top of the stairs telling her, her mother had gone downstairs then she sat up. She began to cry. She knew she would have to tell her mother what she had done and why, but not yet. She dreaded going to school tomorrow. Megan and the others wouldn't let up. They would beat her again. Then she remembered Nora's suggestion, *"Daisy if you like you can stand with us at playtime…"*

"Stand with Nora and her friends," she muttered. Oh if it only works and they leave me alone. Sighing heavily she lay back. Sleep came slowly.

****

Downstairs, Jane studied Patrick. He's always quiet now, she thought. She knew he worried, but she didn't want him to know she was just as worried.

"Jane," said Patrick shortly after the eleven o'clock news finished. "Maybe we should make plans."

"Plans? What do you mean?"

"For the kids, when...when I get...worse."

Jane studied him, then rose and sat on his knees in the arm chair and put her arms around him. "Patrick, we'll get through this. Don't worry. We'll just have to take one day at a time."

"But Jane...why...why me?" cried Patrick burying his head in her breast. "Why does this have to happen to us?"

Jane sighed. She had no answer. She had read all there was to know about Alzheimer's disease or Dementia as it was more commonly known. It was true Patrick was young to have the symptoms, but he had them- he was diagnosed with Alzheimer's disease. There was no cure. The pills would prolong the effects of the terrible disease, but eventually he would need care, expert care, care she might not be able to give him. He would need twenty-four hour care, she would need help. Her husband might have to go into a Nursing Home. And suddenly she too was crying.

7

At break time the following morning Daisy hurried to stand beside Nora, Catherine, Maudie and two other girls. Apparently Nora had told Catherine and Maudie why Daisy was there, because Catherine slapped her gently on the shoulder saying, "Welcome to our gang."

Around five past eleven Danni walked past them.

"O'Hara!" she called. "I want to speak to you. Come here."

Daisy stared at her, her heart pounding with fear.

"No…no…"

"She doesn't want to," said Nora stepping in front of Daisy.

"Who asked you, fat bod?" snapped Danni, her face twisted with anger. "I'm asking O'Hara."

At this Nora turned to Daisy. "Don't be afraid, Daisy," she whispered. "Daisy," she said loudly. "Do you want to speak to Danni…Minogue…?"

Catherine and the other girls began to giggle.

"No," said Daisy moving closer to the bigger girl.

It was just then Jack and Tommy were passing. Jack frowned when he saw who Daisy was with. On the way to school he had tackled his sister about stealing the money, but she had vehemently denied taking it. By the time they got to school he was beginning to believe her. It has to be a mistake, he thought. With all the trouble with daddy, maybe mummy made a mistake.

"You heard her," said Nora. "Now push off."

Catherine and Maudie gasped and took a step back, because for a second or two they thought the furious bully was going to attack Nora. But with an angry snort, Danni strode away. As she did, one of the other girls began to laugh and soon all the girls, including Daisy were laughing.

****

As she sat in class that afternoon, Daisy felt as if a load had been lifted off her shoulders. She concentrated on her lessons and it was only when school was over and she hurried to Jack's class to wait for him that she remembered about the five-pound note. She was determined to tell her mother this evening.

She was standing by P7 classroom door when Megan and Danni came out. Megan spotted the little girl right away. Daisy shrank back. Trembling Megan looked up and down the corridor then with a grunt like a wild animal she suddenly punched Daisy in the nose. It was just then that Nora appeared. As Daisy staggered back against the wall, Nora grabbed Megan by the hair and threw her back almost beside Daisy. The sound of the bully hitting her head against the wall resounded up the corridor.

Just then Jack appeared. He gaped at Nora standing with her fists clenched and then his attention was drawn to Daisy. She was holding her nose and blood was pumping between her fingers.

"What did you do?" he shouted at Nora.

"Jack it wasn't…" began Daisy, almost throwing up as she tasted the blood in her mouth.

"You hit my little sister, you big fat lump!" shouted Jack. "If you were a boy…"

Just then the teacher came out.

"Here what's all this. Get away home with you!" he barked, glaring at Jack. He failed to notice Daisy, who was now holding a handkerchief that Nora gave her, to her nose.

As they walked away, Megan hissed, "I'll get you later, fatso."

Nora glared at her. "Will you? I don't think so. You're not dealing with a little girl now," snapped the big girl. "I hit back."

As Daisy, Jack and Tommy headed for the school gate, Jack looked around at Nora and glared at her.

Daisy didn't want to say anything to Jack whilst Tommy was there, so she waited until they parted at the corner of Blackrock Street.

"We'll get even with that big fat lump tomorrow," said Tommy before walking away. "See you, Jack. See you, Daisy."

"Yes we will," muttered Jack as they headed on down the road. He glanced at Daisy. "Are you all right?"

"Jack, it wasn't Nora who hit me, it was Megan," said Daisy removing the handkerchief and looking to see if there was any fresh blood on it. Her nose had stopped bleeding.

"Megan," exclaimed Jack stopping.

"Yes. Megan, Danni Watson and Elizabeth Downey have been bullying me this past month," said Daisy unable to stop the tears filling her eyes.

"Bullying you?" Jack studied his tearful sister. "Why didn't you tell me?"

"They said they would get me if I told anyone. Jack, I...I stole Mummy's money."

Jack frowned. "I knew you did, but I didn't know why you wanted it. I thought you were doing drugs..."

"Drugs, wise up!" exclaimed Daisy. "Jack," she said quietly. "I have to tell Mummy I stole from her purse. She'll murder me."

Jack smiled. "No she won't. I'll be there. I'll tell her why you did it. She'll understand. You'll see." He frowned. "Then it was Nora who helped you? Who hit you in the nose?"

"Megan."

"Bitch," hissed Jack. He studied his sister. "Come on. I'll create a diversion and you slip upstairs before Mummy sees you and get cleaned up. We'll wait until after tea when Daddy is sleeping to tell her." He smiled. "Don't worry, Daisy. It'll be all sorted this evening."

Daisy studied her big brother and she never felt more like hugging him than she did then. Her steps felt lighter as she walked beside him on down the road.

8

That evening, with her brother by her side, Daisy told her mother all about the bullies, the beatings and stealing the money from her purse. This time Patrick was there.

"You should have told us, love," he said quietly. "We could have done something about it."

"No Daddy, it would only have made things worse. You don't know what the bullies are like. Jack knows." Daisy turned to her brother.

"Even though they're girls," he said, "Nearly everyone fears them." He looked at Daisy. "But I don't, so don't worry about them ever again, Daisy. I'll have a word with them tomorrow." He smiled.

"And don't worry about the money, love," said Jane. "I'll just take a pound a week out of your allowance."

"Thank you, Mummy," sniffed Daisy. Her eyes bubbling with tears.

"What say we all go up to the Swimming Baths, and after we can stop in at MacDonald's," said Patrick smiling.

****

Next morning as they walked to school, after they had met Tommy at the corner, Jack explained to him what had been happening.

Tommy glanced at Daisy. He could understand how she felt. He too was afraid of Megan and the others.

"What are we going to do about Nora the elephant?" he asked.

"Tommy, don't call her that!" snapped Jack. "If it hadn't been for Nora, Daisy might have been badly hurt. From now on, anyone says anything to Nora about her weight or size they'll have me to answer to." He sighed silently. He was going to have to apologize to the big girl and he wasn't looking forward to it.

When they came to the school gate, Megan, Danni, Elizabeth and two other girls were standing there. Danni held her closed fist up to Daisy and she moved closer to Jack.

"I wouldn't do that if I were you, Minogue," snapped Jack. "From now on, leave my sister alone, and if I find out you're bullying any other younger children, I'll report you all to the Head, and don't think I won't!"

"You tell the Head, O'Hara and we'll get you both, you and your sister," snarled Megan.

Jack studied her angry face. It was just then that Nora and Catherine came walking through the gate.

"Here comes fatso Nora!" shouted Elizabeth pointing.

Megan and the other girls began to laugh.

Nora looked at Jack and he looked away, but quickly making up his mind he walked towards her.

"Nora, could I speak to you for a minute?" he said.

"What do you want?" snapped Catherine.

"Just a few words with Nora, if you wouldn't mind, Catherine.

Catherine looked at Nora. She nodded that it was OK.

Daisy watched as Jack and Nora walked into school together, then realizing Megan and Danni were near, she hurried after them.

Megan snarled as she saw Daisy run after her brother and Nora.

"We'll have to do something about them," she whispered to Danni. "If we don't, our funds will dry up. The other girls will defy us."

"What are you going to do?" asked Elizabeth as Megan pulled out her mobile and began ringing a number. As she spoke she moved slightly away from the others.

"Yes, meet us at the corner of the road. Yes after four. Yes."

Megan returned to the others. She was smiling. "Joe and Gallagher are meeting us after school." Suddenly she laughed then began to walk into school. Danni followed her, but Elizabeth stayed slightly behind. Gallagher and Joe, she thought. Oh God not those two.

****

Jack took a deep breath and waited a second or two before speaking.

"Nora, I'd like to apologize for the names I've called you. I realize now what a dickhead I've been. If it hadn't been for you, my sister might have been badly hurt."

"Is that why you're apologizing to me, not because the names you called me were hurtful," said Nora quietly.

Jack saw the tears bubbling in her eyes.

"No…well yes…no," he said feeling stupid. "No, not just that. Anyway, I'm sorry, Nora and thanks."

"No need to thank me. I know what it's like to be bullied. Calling names is a form of bullying. Just because I'm…fa…heavy, that's no reason for anyone to call me, big elephant Nora."

"I…I know. I'm really sorry, Nora. Can't we be…friends?"

Jack looked steadily into the big girl's tearful eyes.

"Friends?" she said quietly. Then she smiled.

Jack couldn't get over how much her face changed when Nora smiled. He couldn't stop his heartbeat pounding. He smiled back, nodded and repeated, "Friends."

Suddenly Nora stuck out her hand.

Daisy smiled as she watched her brother and Nora smiling and shaking hands. She felt happier now than she had felt that whole term.

But it was all to change very soon.

****

On the way home from school, Jack, Daisy, Tommy, Nora and Catherine walked together. It was Tommy who spotted them first.

"Jesus," he hissed nodding.

Jack narrowed his eyes when he saw the three bullies standing with two young men. He recognized one of them, but it was Tommy who whispered his name, "Carlin the Hood."

Everyone knew who Joe Carlin was, a drug dealer and a well-known thug who had been in and out of trouble and prison several times. He wore a short denim jacket with indecipherable writing all over it. His hair was spiked all over and he had a feral quality about him. A cigarette hung from his thin lips the smoke curling up into his flat nose.

The other teenager was short with a bull neck and wore a threadbare black leather Jacket with chains and other ornaments attached to it. On one of his fists he wore a brass knuckle duster.

Jack stopped. "It's obvious they're going to try and frighten us," he whispered. "They won't be able to do anything if we stick together."

"Nora," whispered Catherine. "I'm scared." Suddenly she backed away then turned and crying, "Sorry!" she ran back down the road.

"Catherine!" shouted Nora. "Don't be stupid! Come back!"

"Never mind, Nora," whispered Jack. "We won't back down. We're going this way and we're not turning back. Right?" He glanced at Tommy. His pal's face was as pale as new paper. Jack knew he was scared. But so was he. "It'll be OK, Tommy. We just have to face up to them. Right everyone."

With their hearts pounding, the two boys and two girls walked to the corner of the road.

As they drew nearer to the low wall that separated the road from the broad alleyway, the three bullies stepped into the middle of the footpath blocking their way. It was Megan who spoke first. Ignoring the others she shouted at Daisy. "You thought that was it, did you, you little bitch!" she snarled. "Well now tomorrow you're going to bring us, ten pounds."

Gently pushing to the front of the others Jack shouted, "She's bringing you nothing tomorrow. Your days of bullying are over. I told you, if I hear of any of you bullying Daisy, or anyone, at our school again, I'll report you to the Head."

"I don't think you're going to do that, O'Hara," snarled Carlin, spitting out his cigarette, pushing the girls aside and towering over Jack.

"I...I... will," said Jack trying hard not to show he was terrified of Carlin.

"You won't," hissed Carlin, suddenly grabbing Jack by the throat and forcing him up against the wall. "The girls need money to buy what I supply, you understand?"

"Le...let me go!" shouted Jack struggling to get free of the thug.

"You understand," hissed Carlin, spittle flying from his mouth as he forced Jack harder against the wall.

Jack could feel himself blacking out, but he still struggled. Then...

"Let him go!" shouted a voice.

Startled, the bully glared at Nora who had pushed past Megan and the others and was reaching for his right arm.

Carlin nodded to Megan and the bullies. Grinning, the three teenagers reached for Nora.

Megan was the first to feel the flat handed blow from Nora on her chest. With a gasp she flew back, hitting her head against the wall. Danni, shocked stared at her, only to hear Nora give a sort of squeal and feel a blow to her chest. With her eyes wide with shock she staggered back against Gallagher who so far had said nothing and had done nothing to help Carlin.

Elizabeth gaped at her two friends lying on the ground then looked at Nora who was breathing hard and glaring at Carlin.

"I said, let him go," Nora repeated, her face impassive as she glared at the thug.

Surprised, Carlin released Jack's throat, but still held onto his arms. He studied Nora then glanced at Danni and Megan who were sitting up still recovering from Nora's attack.

"Gallagher," he hissed. "Get that fat bitch!"

Gallagher studied Nora and grinned as she stood with her hands waving about, her feet apart and clucking like a hen. "So you know a bit about martial arts do you." Suddenly he crouched low and waving his hands in front of him and screeching like a cockerel he approached Nora. "Well so do I. Come and feel a bit of Mr. Duster." The brass knuckle duster glinted in the sunlight.

But the big girl stayed where she was still waving her hands around and making hen sounds. She showed no fear.

Suddenly Gallagher dived in and swung his fist at her.

Tommy and Daisy gaped when they saw Nora feint to one side then spin on her two legs one of her feet catching Gallagher on the head. With a sickening thud the drug dealer flew back to slide along the edge of the footpath.

Nora glared at Carlin. "I won't ask you again," she said breathing hard from her efforts.

Now Jack was able to pull free and moved quickly to join Nora and the others.

Carlin studied Nora, looked at Gallagher who was slowly rising to his feet, and then suddenly making up his mind he said, "Let's go. We'll sort them out later."

As Elizabeth helped the furious Megan to her feet, the drug dealers walked away.

"You remember my warning!" shouted Jack. "If I catch you bullying any one from now on, not only will I tell the Head, I'll report you all to the Police!"

At this Carlin turned. With one finger he pointed at Jack. Then he said coldly, "I hear your old man's a beaten docket, O'Hara. It might be better if you kept your mouth shut about us. Something might happen to him. We know where he works and we know where you live!" Then Carlin touched his two eyes and pointed one finger at Jack.

Jack glanced at the others. Carlin's words had frightened him.

****

Later as they all headed home they talked about how Nora had saved them.

"When I was being bullied at school in Japan, my Daddy took me to a martial arts teacher. I learned a few things from him," she explained.

"A few things," exclaimed Tommy admiringly. "You'll have to teach *us*, a few things."

"I was thinner then of course," said Nora. "I only started to eat when… when… my Mummy became sick."

Jack studied Nora again. She's so modest, he thought. She could have whacked me and Tommy anytime, but didn't.

Soon it was time for them all to part. Nora was the last to go and Jack stood with her at the corner while Daisy walked on a little.

"Thanks Nora, and again, I'm sorry about the way me and Tommy behaved."

"No problem," said Nora. "I'd better go." Smiling she walked away.

"I'll see you at school tomorrow!" shouted Jack.

Without turning Nora waved her hand.

As Jack hurried after Daisy he could feel his heart pounding, but then he began to think about the drug dealers and the bullies. It would be too easy if it was all over, he thought. They'll not give up. He frowned as he thought about Carlin's threat to his father.

****

That evening something happened after tea. Jack was in the kitchen texting Nora and telling her all about his father and how ill he was. Daisy was just coming out of her bed room when she saw her father walking up the stairs. He stopped and stared at her.

"Mary," he exclaimed. "What are you doing here? You should be at school."

Daisy gaped at her father. "Daddy what are you talking about?"

"Mary, sure you know mam will be angry. Now go on, get your schoolbag and get off…" Her father frowned as he stared at Daisy.

"Mummy! Mummy!" cried Daisy. She was frightened. She studied her father. He was standing with a big frown on his face.

Just then her mother appeared. What is it?"

"Mummy, Daddy was calling me, Mary," said Daisy. She was almost in tears. My daddy didn't know who I was, she thought.

Jane sized up the situation quickly and whispered, "That's OK, Daisy. Go on into your room. I'll see to Daddy."

Daisy watched from her bedroom door as her mother led Patrick downstairs.

"I…I really thought she was my sister, Mary," came her daddy's words.

Crying now, Daisy went into her bedroom. It was at least ten minutes later before her mother came in. She could see that Daisy had been crying.

"Daisy," she said quietly taking her hands and sitting on the bed. "You know your Daddy's illness makes him forget things…"

"Yes," said Daisy softly, unable to stop the big tear slipping down her pale face. "But he said he would never forget us…me." She sniffed.

As Jane held her daughter she thought about how quickly Patrick's dementia had taken hold of him. He's much worse, she thought. She worried now for him, herself and the children.

9

Next day, on the way to school, Daisy told Jack what had happened the night before, about her father and how he had mistaken her for their Aunt Mary when she was young.

"Daisy," said Jack. "I've been looking more into Daddy's illness on the Internet. Our Daddy won't get any better. There's no cure for Alzheimer's Disease."

"No cure, but maybe…maybe…" began Daisy tearfully.

Jack could see his little sister was upset, but she has to know, he thought. "Daisy, Daddy will forget, everything, our names. He'll even forget who Mummy is…"

"Mummy!"

"Yes. Alzheimer's is a deg…degen….degenerative disease."

"What does that mean?"

"It's a disease that attacks the brain. All Daddy's memories will go, even how his brain works, everything, until there will come a time when he won't even be able to speak or move his arms or legs."

Jack gulped as he studied Daisy. He wished now he had included her in everything- snorkeling and stuff. He wished she had come with them on the day they saw the Porpoise. It was a memory he would always have. He wished he could have shared it with his little sister.

"Will...will it happen fast? I mean, how long does Daddy have before he forgets about us completely?" asked Daisy.

"That's just it, Daisy. There's no time limit. Some people live with Alzheimer's for a long time, others it's quick. I don't know how long it will be before Daddy has to go into a wheelchair or to...to...a Home."

"A Home?" exclaimed Daisy. "But he has a Home."

"Not that kind of home- a Home for the disabled, a Nursing Home."

"Disabled?" whispered Daisy. "Jack, I'm frightened. I'm frightened for Daddy."

Jack sighed. "So am I, and for Mummy as well."

Just then they reached the school gates. Tommy, Nora, Catherine and Maudie were waiting for them.

"We'll both just have to look after Daddy until then, eh," said Jack smiling at Daisy.

Daisy nodded. Out of the corner of her eye she saw Megan and the others watching them. She stayed close to her brother as they walked to the entrance to the classrooms.

****

At break-time they all gathered together near the far wall. From there they had a good view of the whole playground.

"Nora, tell us more about Japan and what happened?" said Tommy.

Nora looked at Jack. "There's nothing really to tell. I was being bullied, by four bigger girls from a class above me. Three of them were

Europeans. They terrified the whole school- even the teachers were frightened of them. Anyway, after I got beat up, Daddy took me to a friend of his who was a martial arts teacher. I learned quickly because I was frightened and I didn't want to be frightened anymore." She looked at Daisy. "It's not nice being afraid of someone."

Daisy nodded.

"Then what?" asked Catherine. "Did you beat the shit out of them?"

Nora smiled and Tommy guffawed.

"I fought back, but even then I got another beating. I was hurt real bad." Nora looked away. "Daddy went to the Head, but when he could get no satisfaction out of him he went to the newspapers. The following week after I had recovered and was strong enough, I went back to school, at my own request. You see all that week I had been thinking about what they had done, were doing. Other children were suffering. It had to be stopped. I spent almost the whole week training and practicing some Kung-Fu moves. Anyway when they tackled me again I sort of went mad…"

"Mad," giggled Tommy.

"Yes. I beat the four of them up, broke the arms of two of the bullies. Three of them had to be admitted to hospital."

"Hospital?" muttered Maudie staring at Nora.

"It got into the newspapers and I was considered somewhat of a heroine. Mothers, and some children, wrote to the newspaper telling the editor how they had been bullied and how when they heard what I'd done they admired me for it." Nora shrugged. "Four months later Daddy brought us home to England."

Suddenly they all looked across the playground when they heard a squeal.

A little girl was being pinned up against the wall by Megan and her gang- somehow a fourth bigger girl had joined them.

"Well," hissed Jack starting to walk across the playground. "Are we going to do something about that?

Tommy looked at Maudie and Catherine and followed by Nora and Daisy they hurried to the far side of the playground.

"We want two pounds tomorrow," Megan was snarling into the frightened girl's face. "and don't…"

"Leave her alone!" shouted Jack grabbing the violent girl by the arm.

Megan shrugged him off. As she did, the little girl, crying, ran past her.

"I warned you," shouted Jack.

"Listen O'Hara, Carlin and Gallagher aren't too happy with you. They told us to tell you if you don't butt out, they're going to do your father."

Jack glared at the bigger girl. Her nose ring seemed to grow bigger.

Suddenly without a word he strode away.

Daisy, Nora, Tommy and the other girls gaped after him.

Daisy frowned as she looked at Megan and Danni. They were grinning.

"Bottled out, didn't he?" snarled Danni taking a step towards Daisy.

"Leave her," snapped Nora, pulling Daisy away.

As they walked away, they heard the jeers from Megan and her gang.

Nora looked for Jack, but he was nowhere in sight.

****

Ten minutes later they were all in class. Nora looked for Jack but he wasn't there. Fifteen minutes later he came in.

"You're late," said the teacher.

"Sorry sir," said Jack then walked to his seat.

Megan and Danni sneered at him as he walked past.

Five minutes later a boy knocked at the classroom door, went to Mr. Thompson and handed him a note. Thompson read it and said, "Thank you."

Thompson looked down the classroom. "Megan Heaney, Danni Watson, Elizabeth Downey, you're all to report to the Head's office."

With a frown Megan rose to her feet. Elizabeth stared at Danni.

"At once!" snapped Mr. Thompson.

Nora glanced over at Jack as the three bullies hurried out of the classroom.

****

Half an hour later the three girls returned. As Megan passed Jack's desk she hissed, "I'll get you, bastard."

Jack shrugged.

****

As they walked home, Jack told the others what he had done.

"I said I'd report them and I have. The Head said she would give them a warning."

"Do you think they'll heed it?" asked Maudie. "That Megan is crazy. She'll not listen to anyone."

"If they're caught bullying again they'll be out," said Jack.

"Out? You mean expelled? Jesus," exclaimed Catherine.

"They deserve it," said Tommy. "Remember wee Joan Moore, last year. She tried to top herself. They found out she was being bullied. She never told who it was, but we all knew."

Daisy frowned. She could understand how Joan felt. She had felt so utterly helpless, not even able to tell Jack or her parents.

"Do you think there are other children being bullied in other schools?" asked Maudie.

"Probably," said Jack frowning. Other children being bullied, he thought. There has to be. His frown grew deeper as he headed into class with the others.

****

That evening their mother told them that their daddy had had to leave his work, he was now on disablement leave.

At tea everyone was quiet. Jack was thinking about other children being bullied, Jane was thinking, what am I going to do? Patrick will be at home every day. She knew it wouldn't help his illness not to be able to do his work. She knew he loved his job, had loved his job.

When tea was over, Jack and Daisy washed the dishes. When they were done, Jack said, "Daddy, can I use your computer for an hour?"

"May you use my computer," corrected his father, "of course you may? Have you an assignment to do for school?"

"No, it's just something I want to look up." He turned to Daisy. "Would you like to come with me?"

Daisy frowned. Usually Jack didn't want to include her in anything.

****

When the computer was booted up, Jack punched in the word, "Bullying."

For over an hour they read about the many children who had been bullied and who were being bullied. Some of them had committed suicide or attempted to, their bullying was so extreme. When they had digested much of the information Jack said, "Daisy, what are we going to do?"

"We? What do you mean?"

"We just can't stand idly by and do nothing. My God, Daisy, look what you went through and I didn't even know about it. It was horrible. I'll never forgive myself for not being aware."

Daisy sniffed back a tear. But she was wondering what her brother meant. *"We just can't stand idly by and do nothing."*

Later as Jack switched off the computer she noticed he was smiling.

"What is it, Jack?"

"I'll tell you all about it tomorrow when I speak to the others. I'd better text Nora. I promised to go for a walk with her later on."

As they hurried into the sitting room Daisy was wondering what put her brother in a good mood.

10

At break time that morning Jack and the others stood at their usual place in the playground.

"We would need a website," said Nora after Jack had explained what he was going to do.

"And a web-mail address for the children to contact," said Tommy.

"Then we need to get the information about our website out to the other schools in the Town," said Maudie. She smiled. She was excited.

"I could do up the website," said Nora. "I helped my Daddy do his when he set up his small internet business."

"My Daddy can help too," said Jack, hoping his daddy could.

"My Uncle Freddy works for one of the local newspapers. He might be interested enough to do a piece about what we're doing," said Maudie.

Jack looked around at everyone. He smiled. They were all in.

"Right, we have to have a proper meeting. Can – could all of you come to my house on Saturday? We can have a meeting in our garage to discuss any other ideas. I'll explain to my Mummy and Daddy what we're meeting about."

"I can make it," said Nora.

"Me too," said Catherine.

"And me," said Tommy.

They all looked at Maudie.

"I'll be there. What time?"

"Make it about ten-thirty," said Jack.

As they all headed into class everyone was buzzing with excitement.

****

That Saturday morning Jane showed them all into the sitting room. The evening before Jack had explained to his parents what he was trying to do. They felt very proud of him.

After tea and biscuits, Jack led the others into the garage. Earlier, he had rid away some old boxes and other stuff to make room for the meeting.

Daisy sat on an old computer box beside Tommy. Nora sat on a wonky swivel chair. Maudie and Catherine sat on two wooden chairs that had been up in the garage attic ever since Jack and his family had come to live in their house.

Tommy grinned as he looked around. "The first meeting of the Bully Squad," he said.

Everyone looked at each other and smiled.

"By the way, I've made up a rap for it," said Tommy, his face beaming. "Do you want to hear it?"

Jack looked at Nora and grinned. "Go ahead, Tommy."

Tommy licked his lips and smiling began. *"When you're feeling down and things look bad. Who ya gonna call? The Bully Squad. If you're being bullied, can't tell your dad. Who ya gonna call? The Bully Squad."* Tommy smiled as he looked at the others then shouted, "Who ya gonna call?"

Everyone, including Daisy, who couldn't help being overexcited, shouted, "The Bully Squad!"

Maudie and Catherine looked at each other and smiled.

"That's as much as I've done with the rap," said Tommy modestly. "But I'll add to it when the muse comes." He laughed aloud at this.

"Jack," said Nora seriously. "I was thinking, first we should do up some flyers and distribute them around the school. Put a big one up on the notice board about what we intend to do."

"Flyers?" said Tommy frowning. "What would we say on them?"

"Just to inform everyone at our school that there is someone to help them, someone they can contact. To say that we are intending to have a website for children being bullied up and running soon," said Nora

"That's a terrific idea," said Jack.

****

While they were busy planning their strategy, on the far side of town, Matthew Carson was being approached by his next door neighbor, Mr. Doherty.

Matthew was a broad shouldered, fourteen years old who loved football, in particular Manchester United, and was one of the most popular boys at St. Patrick's college. He also played for the school team and was considered by Mr. Gregory, the PT assistant, to be one of the most promising players he had coached.

"It's our wee Robbie," said his neighbor.

Matthew had been trimming the back hedge when his middle-aged neighbor had called through the hedge asking him could he have a few words. Puzzled, because Matthew had hardly ever spoken to Mr. Doherty, he climbed down the rickety wooden steps and walked to the small hole in the dividing hedge. Matthew knew Robbie Doherty, Mr. Doherty's only son, slightly. One day he had walked to school with him. Robbie was a quiet, thoughtful boy, thin with a pale face.

"Robbie!" Matthew's frown grew deeper. "What about him?"

Mr. Doherty looked left and right then behind to the house. "I've found out about the bullying."

Matthew frowned. Is he saying I'm bullying his son? he thought.

"Look Mr. Doherty, I…"

"There are four of them," said Mr. Doherty. "They're from over at the Gobnascale Housing Estate. They hurt wee Robbie last week."

Matthew stared at the tears bubbling in his neighbor's eyes. He listened, wondering all throughout the conversation why Mr. Doherty was telling him about it.

"Their leader is a boy called, Ian Smith."

"Smith, Ian Smith." Matthew knew Smith. He was in the school team. He played center-half and once he had broken the leg of a winger on one of the opposing teams. Smith had gotten away with it, but Matthew and several other members of the school team knew he had done it on purpose.

"They beat up Robbie last week. Robbie made us promise not to tell the Head Master, but it's… hard. He begged us not to tell, but Smith and his gang, they're still bullying him."

"Are they?" said Matthew looking up at the sky. Black clouds were drifting over the back of the estate. He wondered would he have time to finish cutting the hedge. His father had warned him about using the electric hedge-cutter when it was raining.

"Yes," said Mr. Doherty.

Matthew studied him. He was still wondering why Mr. Doherty was telling him all this.

"Matthew... er... I was wondering if you could keep an eye out for him?"

"Me? An eye?" Matthew's frown deepened even more. "But Mr. Doherty...I..."

"I'll pay you."

"What?"

"Ten pounds. Just to look after him in the playground and going to and coming home from school," said Mr. Doherty looking back at the house again. "Ten pounds a week."

"Mr. Doherty, I...wouldn't...I... don't..." Matthew didn't know what to say. "I couldn't take any money..."

"Then you'll do it?" exclaimed Mr. Doherty, a smile lighting up his somber face.

"No... I..."

"Look, Matthew I understand your position, but you look like a lad who can handle himself..."

"Handle myself?" Matthew knew he was able to take care of himself. Ever since his mother had run off with a colleague who worked with her in the council, it had been Matthew and his father. He had rebelled at first, but with the help of a kindly aunt and Sinead, he had learned to cope, that it wasn't his fault his mother had left them. Back then he had gotten into several fights, one of them had been with Smith. He had bloodied his nose and the bully had backed off. They hadn't spoken since, on or off the pitch.

"If you could just walk to school with Robbie and back home again. Keep an eye out for him in the playground, I'll pay you. Ten pounds a week. Look, if it isn't enough, I'll…"

"Mr. Doherty, it's not the money." Matthew thought now about walking to school in the morning. He always made the detour to his girlfriend, Sinead's house and walked to school with her. They usually walked home together. It was just then his mobile rang. He knew who it was before looking, Sinead. He swore to her several times that she was psychic. Sinead was from Derry, Northern Ireland and her family had come to live in England two years ago to escape the Troubles. He loved her accent, he loved more than her accent.

"I'd better answer this," he said.

"Matthew will you do it?"

The mobile rang again, Robbie William's, "Angel" tune irritatingly loud. He made a mental note to change it.

"Do it?"

"Walk with Robbie to school and back, protect him. It'll only be for a while until the bullies move on to someone else."

Matthew studied Mr. Doherty's face trying to understand what it would be like if he had a son who was being bullied by Smith and his gang. He couldn't walk him to school every day or pick him up after school, or watch out for him in the playground. He knew Mr. Doherty worked for the council.

"Please, Matthew," pleaded Mr. Doherty. "I'm really desperate here."

The mobile kept ringing.

"I'll... I'll see," said Matthew. "Now if you'll excuse me, I do have to answer this. I was expecting an important call," he lied.

"Yes, yes, thanks Matthew. I'll send Robbie around Monday morning."

Matthew stared through the hedge as Mr. Doherty hurried to the house. "I didn't say I would do it," he muttered, then, "Hi."

"Where were you?" asked the quiet voice.

"Talking to Mr. Doherty, our neighbor."

"What's the craic?" asked Sinead.

"His son, Robbie is being bullied."

"Robbie? What are you on about?"

"Our next door neighbor, Mr. Doherty. He wants me to walk his son, Robbie to school every day and pick him up after, and walk home with him."

"What? Why?"

"Smith and his lot are bullying him," said Matthew.

"Ian Smith...Matthew maybe you shouldn't get involved. Smith's a bit of a nutter. You know what he's like..."

"I know."

"Are you going to do it?"

"I might. Sure it'll only be for a week or two, so Mr. Doherty says, until Smith moves on to someone else. He offered me a tenner."

"Ten quid? Are you going to take it?"

"What do you think? Of course not."

Matthew thought about the money. He could have used it. He needed a new pair of football boots- he'd have to settle for new studs instead. His father had already told him he couldn't afford to buy him new boots, even though he encouraged him to play.

"Are we on for tonight?" asked Sinead.

"Sure." Matthew frowned. "On? Where?"

"Oh, for heaven's sake, Matthew. The club…Drama…Remember…Duh…"

Matthew laughed. "You think I'm dumb, do you?"

Sinead laughed. "No, just thick."

"Wait'll I get my hands on you tonight."

"You keep your hands to yourself, Matthew Carson," laughed Sinead. "Look I have to go. I'll see you around seven-thirty, OK?"

"It's a date." said Matthew. He was about to say, love you, in reply to Sinead's "Love you," but closed his mobile instead.

He stared up at the hedge. I'd better hurry, he thought. The black clouds were gathering quickly above the town.

****

It was twenty past one in the afternoon when the meeting ended and the newly formed; "Bully Squad" had a rough plan of what was needed. Jack was to do up the flyers on his father's computer and print at least two hundred.

Maudie was to contact her uncle and hopefully get him to write a few words about the Bully Squad in his paper.

Nora would do up a rough website and later show the others what she had done. Then she had to organize their email address. They had all agreed what it would be- www.thebullysquad.co.uk.

****

Early next morning Jack's father answered the door. Mr. Doherty was standing there, and beside him stood his son, looking very embarrassed.

"Can I help…?" he began. But Matthew was there behind him.

"It's OK, Dad. Robbie is walking to school with me today."

"He is?" Matthew's father frowned.

"Thanks Matthew," said Mr. Doherty. "Mr. Carson," he said, touching his forehead then he turned and hurried away.

"Hi Robbie, come on in," said Matthew. "I won't be long. Have you had your breakfast yet?"

The little boy nodded. Robbie was small for a boy of eleven. He had long brown hair and wore glasses, his second pair that month, as one of Smith's cronies had stamped on the last pair. He stood awkwardly by the table as Matthew wolfed down his cornflakes.

Five minutes later they were walking down the road heading for Sinead's house.

"Your dad tells me that Smith and his gang gave you a beating last week?"

Robbie frowned. "Yes, in the playground."

"What did they want? Money?"

"Yes. I tried to stand up to them, but they were too big," said Robbie in a small voice. "I told my Daddy. He wanted to go to the Head. But that would only have made things worse."

Matthew studied the little boy's pale face. Big tears bubbled on Robbie's eyes. "I was afraid," he added.

That Smith needs a lesson or two, thought Matthew, his fist hardening. He felt sorry for the little boy.

Shortly they were approaching the corner of the road and there she stood, Sinead. His heart leaped when he saw her. She had always had that effect on him, ever since the first day she had walked into the classroom. At first he had deliberately stayed away from her, he didn't know why, he was afraid of the effect she had on him, but gradually it happened. At the school dance she had stayed with him all night and that was it. She was his girlfriend.

"Hi," she greeted, her beautiful face lighting up when she smiled. "You must be, Robbie." She bent to shake the little boy's hand. "I'm Sinead."

"Hello Sinead," said Robbie, his face growing red.

Matthew grinned.

As they walked on they discussed the bully and his gang.

"Matthew, we should get some of the others to help us," said Sinead. "When they find out what has happened to Robbie they'll help us. Smith and his gang are too much for you, us."

"Us?" said Matthew grinning. "And what are you going to do, hit him over the head with your handbag?" He laughed.

Robbie smiled when Sinead gave Matthew a heavy thump on the shoulder. "I'll hit you over the head, funny man," exclaimed Sinead smiling.

As they approached the school gate a group of teenagers were standing near the two pillars. Among them were Smith and two of his gang.

When Smith saw Matthew and Sinead with Robbie walking between them he scowled. He stepped out in front of them. He pointed at Robbie. "I want a word with you, Doherty," he snarled, grinding his teeth.

Robbie shrank back.

"He doesn't want a word with you, Smith," said Matthew, reaching to hold Robbie by the shoulder and stepping to go around the bigger teenager.

Smith frowned then suddenly grabbed Robbie by the coat pulling him away from Matthew and Sinead. As he did so he pulled Robbie against Sinead and she tripped over the little boy's legs.

Matthew, with his face blazing with anger grabbed Smith by the arm. "Smith, leave him!" he shouted.

Surprised Smith released Robbie who ran to stand beside Sinead.

With a cry Smith swung a fist at Matthew. The broad-shouldered teenager blocked the punch and pushed Smith away.

"Smith!" shouted Matthew. "I said leave it, and leave Robbie alone! He's with me and Sinead!"

"You and Sinead," hissed Smith looking around. A small group of boys and girls had gathered around them. "You and that Irish bitch deserve each other."

Matthew, anger written all over his face was about to attack Smith when Sinead shouted, "Matthew, no!"

Just then one of the teacher's came walking past. He stopped. "What's all this?"

"Nothing, sir," said Matthew. Giving Smith a cool look he walked towards Robbie and Sinead. Then without looking back, the three of them walked into school.

****

At the same time Jack was speaking to Miss Curtis. "Miss, would it be OK if I put up this notice?"

The Head Teacher frowned. "Notice? What is it?"

Jack handed it to her. The teacher read it, her face creasing slowly into a smile. She handed it back to Jack. "Jack, that's a very good idea. Of course you may put it up. I commend you… and the Bully Squad." She frowned. "I hope there will be no trouble because of it."

"I can't see how there could be," said Jack as he pressed the pins onto the corner of his page. "Miss would it be OK if we passed out some leaflets at break-time?"

"About the Bully Squad?"

"Yes."

"Sure and Jack…"

"Yes miss?"

"It's a wonderful idea. If there is any other help you need please don't be afraid to ask."

As she walked away Miss Curtis was smiling. There's hope for the young yet, she thought.

****

At the break, Jack and the others quickly passed out their leaflets. The conversation was all about the Bully Squad. Some of the younger kids were running around the playground chanting, "Who ya gonna call? The Bully Squad!"

Over near the gate Megan was reading one of the leaflets. With a curse she crumpled up the paper and threw it on the ground and crunched it into the asphalt. She looked across at Daisy who was standing with Nora and the others. They were all laughing, excited and in good spirits.

"We have to do something about this," she snarled.

"What?" snapped Danni. "We daren't start on any of them now. Megan, what are we going to do? We need money."

"I don't know," said Megan. "But tonight when we meet Carlin and Gallagher for some stuff, we can ask them if they can help. That Jack O'Hara needs a lesson. If we don't stop this now, we're buggered." She snarled as she studied Daisy. She thinks she's safe, does she? Well we'll see." Grinding her teeth and clenching her fists she trembled with anger.

11

That evening Nora showed Jack the website she had done up. Jack called his father and Patrick studied what Nora had made up. He offered a few suggestions then went into a blank stare.

Nora frowned as Jack called for his mother.

Later, when they were finished discussing all the options children could take, they went downstairs to the sitting room.

When they got there Patrick was dozing on the sofa beside Daisy who had her arm linked into his.

"Finished?" said Jane rising.
"Not quite. We've a bit to do yet," said Jack.
"Would you like a cup of tea, Nora?" asked Jane.
"No thanks, Mrs. O'Hara, I'd better get home. I've my homework to do," said Nora.
"I'll walk you," said Jack.

Jane followed them to the door. She smiled as she watched her son and Nora walk down the street. She raised her eyes when she saw Jack reach to take Nora's hand. "Hmmm," she said smiling as she went inside.

****

Thirty minutes later Jack was on his way home again. He was just passing the side entrance to Murphy's furniture store when Carlin stepped out onto the footpath in front of him. A blow from behind from Gallagher and the shocked teenager was forced into the entrance.

"Now O'Hara," snarled Carlin forcing Jack hard against the wall by the lapels of his coat. "We have something to ask you and we're not going to ask you politely."

Suddenly Gallagher pulled Carlin to one side and punched Jack hard in the stomach.

With a gasp Jack doubled up. Carlin grabbed him again forcing his head sideways against the wall. "We are asking you politely now, stop this campaign."

"Ca…campaign?" gasped Jack.

"This, Bully Squad thing. Megan and the others don't like it, and neither do we," snarled Gallagher kicking Jack in the small of his back.

With a cry Jack sank to the ground. Suddenly Carlin kicked him on the side of the head and dazed he fell to the ground. As he lay there he thought about Megan and her friends. If they stopped the bully campaign now the three bullies would have a free hand. No child would be safe, especially Daisy.

"No," he gasped. "I won't do it. I…"

Suddenly Carlin dragged him to his feet.

"What did you say?"

"I said I…"

With a curse Gallagher punched him in the face. Another punch from Carlin sent Jack flying against the wall and he slid to the ground. Dazed he looked up.

"If we don't hear you've stopped this bully campaign, the next time we won't be so lenient with you. Don't forget your old man is sick, and Megan and the others could really hurt your little sister." He turned to Gallagher. "Let's go. I think he understands what we mean."

Laughing the two thugs walked away. By then Jack had passed out.

****

On the way home on Friday night from Drama lessons, Matthew and Sinead were passing the Roxy Cinema. Sinead gave a start when she saw Smith and five of his cronies come out through the big glass doors. One of the teenagers pulled the tab on a can of beer. Another was raising a beer to his mouth. At the same time Smith saw Sinead and Matthew. He whispered something to the others and they hurried after Sinead and Matthew.

"Wait up, Carson!" hailed Smith.

Turning, Matthew frowned when Smith and the others surrounded them. One of the teenagers pushed Sinead to one side.

Angry Matthew shouted, "Hey, what do you think you're doing?"

"Never mind about that," hissed Smith pushing his face into Matthew's. "Who gave you the right to protect that wee skitter, Doherty. He's ours."

Matthew gritted his teeth. "Yours," he said angrily. "He's only a wee boy. You've been bullying him and taking money off him. That makes you a big man does it?"

Smith glared. "I'm bigger than you."

Matthew clenched his fists. He knew he didn't have much of a chance against all of the bullies. But if he could make Smith fight him on his own then he did have a chance.

"Prove it, Smith, me and you," said Matthew. "A fair fight, right now."

Smith could feel his heart pounding. He was afraid. He glanced at the others then winked to Joey Simpson a burly red haired teenager. "A fair fight, he says. OK, Carson."

Suddenly he head butted Matthew. With blood spurting from his nose Matthew staggered back. Sinead screamed with fear as Smith attacked Matthew punching him on the face and stomach. But somehow Matthew stayed on his feet. To stop Smith's attack Matthew suddenly clasped his arms around the bigger teenager's body holding on tightly until he could get his breath. Staggering around, they hit the wall by the cinema side entrance and fell. This caused Matthew to let go. He was on his feet before Smith and when the bigger teenager scrambled to his feet Matthew was into him, punching and forcing Smith back. Blood flew everywhere.

As Smith's head was rocked back by a punch from Matthew, Simpson saw that Smith was getting the worst of it. With a curse he dived into Matthew's back and punched him hard. Matthew moaning fell to his knees. With a cry of triumph Smith put the boot in, kicking him in the face. Dazed Matthew staggered back and fell. Immediately Smith and Simpson began kicking him. One heavy kick hit Matthew's right ankle.

Sinead, horrified, leaped on Smith's back and began to claw at his face. As she did she screamed as loud as she could. People coming out of the cinema began to run towards them.

"Smith," shouted Simpson. "Let's get outta here!"

With a curse Smith reached behind for Sinead and pulled her roughly from his back and threw her on the ground. With another curse he kicked her in the ribs.

As the four bullies ran away, Sinead crawled towards Matthew. He was out cold.

12

With a groan, Matthew woke. He looked around. A teenager in the bed opposite him raised his body to see if he was all right.

Matthew looked around the ward. He was in hospital.

"Are...are you OK?" asked the teenager.

"I...I think so," said Matthew. He studied the other boy's face. Both his eyes were black. "What happened to you?"

"I was beat up," answered Jack.

"Me to," said Matthew, trying to smile. His face ached as did his ribs. He could feel his swollen ankle. He was about to ask Jack how long he was here when Jack's mother and father and Daisy entered.

"Jack, oh Jack!" cried Jane. "Who did it?"

Daisy couldn't stop tears filling her eyes when she saw how badly beaten her brother was.

Jack studied his father. He looked OK. He didn't want to worry his parents, not now, not when they had his father's illness to worry about.

"It doesn't matter," he said.

"Doesn't matter!" cried his mother. "Jack, look at you." She frowned. "Has this to do with that bullying campaign?"

"Yes...no...Mum look, I'm OK. Don't worry." He tried to smile. He tried to wink at Daisy to put her at ease, but only succeeded in making his face look more grotesque.

Patrick looked across at Matthew. He smiled. "How are you, son?"

"OK," said Matthew. He was about to tell Mr. O'Hara what happened when Sinead came in, followed by his father.

Jack looked across as they gathered around Matthew's bed.

"The bullying has to stop," he heard Matthew's father say. "They hit Sinead as well."

Later, when they had all gone, Jack and Matthew began to tell each other about how they were fighting the bullies.

"If you can get some leaflets to me I'll pass them around our school," said Matthew. He groaned as he tried to sit up further.

For the next hour they discussed their fight against the bullies. Matthew expressed his admiration for Jack and his bullying campaign. "I hope you'll make me a member of the Bully Squad," he said smiling.

"No problem," said Jack, grinning then wincing with pain.

About five minutes to visiting time Nora, Maudie and Tommy came in. They were horrified when Jack told them who had beaten him.

"They have to be stopped," said Tommy. He was afraid, but at the same time angry at what had happened to his pal.

"It was Megan and the others who were responsible," said Jack. "Carlin and Gallagher will get theirs someday. But we have to show them we won't be frightened off." His next words had the girls gasping. "I'm going to school on Monday…"

"What?" exclaimed Tommy gaping at his pal, "Jack, look at you, your ribs, your face…"

"We have to show the bullies how determined we are, Tommy," said Jack groaning as he tried to ease into a more comfortable position. "We have to show them we won't be cowed down."

"They'll never let you out of the Hossie before Monday," said Maudie.

"They will," said Jack. He looked around the others. "They will."

Tommy looked across at Matthew. "What happened to him?"

Jack said one word. "Bullies."

Just then Nora came in. She tried not to gasp when she saw Jack's face.

"Are…are…you…?"

Jack tried to smile.

"Nora, he says he's going to school on Monday. He has cracked ribs and look at his face," exclaimed Tommy. "Maybe you can talk some sense into him?"

"Tommy, look I'll be OK," said Jack. He smiled at Nora. "It's nice to see you."

She smiled back.

"Nora," said Jack nodding to Matthew. "The rest of you, I'd like you to meet Matthew Carson. Bullies beat him up too."

Nora nodded to Matthew. Tommy walked over to Matthew's bed.

"Nora, maybe if you're coming tomorrow you could bring some leaflets to give to him to distribute around his school," said Jack.

"No problem," said Nora. "Would it be OK if I called at your house and get some printed up?"

"I'll let my Mum know when she visits this evening," said Jack.

Just then the bell rang to inform visitors visiting time was up.

Ten minutes later Jack and Matthew were in the ward on their own.

"You really going to school on Monday?" asked Matthew.

Jack nodded then groaned, the movement making his ribs ache.

Matthew grinned. "You're crazy."

"I know, said Jack, giving a quick laugh, the movement making him groan again. Then he said, "Matthew, you don't mind us giving you the leaflets?"

"Not at all. But I was thinking, Jack, the other schools in the town. The bullies in those schools should be stopped too. Did you hear about the wee boy over at St Patrick's?"

"No."

"It was about two years ago. His mother found him hanging in their garage. He left a note telling her he couldn't go on. He was being bullied by some older girls, imagine, girls."

Jack sighed.

****

On Sunday evening he told his mother he was going home. He told her why. For several minutes she argued with him, but she could see he was determined. She didn't tell Jack about Patrick losing his temper and shouting at her and Daisy during dinner.

Before leaving that evening Jack went over to Matthew. A Pile of leaflets left in the afternoon by Nora sat on his bedside locker.

"Matthew, you have my number and email. When you're out we have to get together."

Matthew watched Jack, who was almost bent over, leave the ward. Now he worried. Sinead was going to school with Robbie tomorrow. He had begged her not to. But she was determined Smith was not going to hurt Robbie. He smiled now as he thought about her. She had stayed long after visiting time was over.

He lifted his bed sheet and stared down at his ankle. It was still very swollen. If he had been able to walk he too would have gone to school. Smith and his cronies had to be beaten. He gritted his teeth now as he thought about the bully. He knew they would fight again. This time the bully wouldn't win.

13

"Is Robbie ready, Mr. Doherty?" asked Sinead.

Mr. Doherty gaped at the slim girl. "Ready?" He looked past her for Matthew. "For what?"

"To go to school, I'm taking him today," said Sinead smiling.

Just then Robbie appeared. He stared at Sinead. He had just heard her.

"Wh… where's Matthew?"

"He's in hospital," said Sinead. "He asked me to bring you to school."

"You," exclaimed Mr. Doherty and his son together. They looked at each other.

"Matthew should be out on Wednesday. He asked me to fill in for him until then…"

"But the bullies?" exclaimed Robbie's father.

Sinead smiled. "Don't worry, Mr. Doherty. Robbie will be safe with me."

Mr. Doherty stared at his son. "Are you OK with this…?" he asked.

Robbie studied Sinead. "Ye…yes…I….I think so." He had quickly gotten to like the Irish girl on their way to and from school.

"Don't worry," said Sinead again. "Are you ready, Robbie?"

A couple of minutes later Mr. Doherty was staring after Sinead and his son as they walked down the street. He shook his head. What could he do? He had to believe the girl knew what she was doing.

****

Around the same time, Jack, Nora and the others were approaching the school gate. Leaning on Nora's arm, Jack was gasping with pain and walking very slowly.

Megan, Danni and Elizabeth were standing near the classroom entrance when Jack and the others approached them.

Everyone stared at Jack. Realizing this, Jack stopped and looked around. Then in a loud voice he shouted, "The bullies won't stop me or the Bully Squad! Never be afraid of bullies because they're cowards!"

Suddenly Tommy began to do his rap. *"When you're feeling down and things look bad. Who ya gonna call? The Bully Squad! If you're being bullied, can't tell your dad. Who ya gonna call? The Bully Squad!"* Tommy looked around. "I said, who ya gonna call?"

Jack almost cried when he heard everyone around him shout- **"THE BULLY SQUAD!"**

"Who ya gonna call?" screamed Tommy.

"THE BULLY SQUAD!" screamed everyone around him.

Daisy's heart almost burst through her chest when she heard Tommy shout again, "Who ya gonna call?" And everyone around shouted louder, **"The Bully Squad!"**

Smiling, Jack walked past Megan and her cronies and followed by Tommy and the others headed into class.

"What are we going to do now?" hissed Danni.

"How the hell would I know?" shouted Megan pushing her aside and walking through the door.

****

Across town, Smith and the others were standing by the school gates. One of Smith's eyes widened when he saw Sinead approaching with Robbie by her side. The bully's right eye was swollen and almost closed. Now, with his lip curling with anger, he stepped in front of Sinead as they came to the school gates. Other pupils moved out of the way and walked around them. Robbie moved closer to Sinead.

"Doherty, come here," hissed Smith.

"No Robbie, stay where you are," said Sinead moving in front of the terrified little boy.

Smith glared at Robbie. "Did you hear what I said, Doherty?" he hissed through clenched teeth.

"He heard you, Smith, and he doesn't want to!" shouted Sinead attracting the attention of several other girls standing nearby.

Smith made a grab at Robbie, but Sinead was ready for him. With her fist bunched she punched the bully full in the face. With a shocked gurgle he staggered back.

"Did you hear me?" screamed Sinead.

It was then that some girls gathered behind Sinead.

Smith glared at Sinead and pointed a finger at Robbie. "We'll get you, Doherty!" he shouted. "And you, I.R.A. bitch!"

"No you won't, Smith," shouted Sinead. "It took five of you to leave Matthew in hospital at the week-end!" Sinead was aware of the gasps of the girls behind her. "Matthew won't be on his own again." She turned to the girls. Several of them nodded.

Smith snarled as he looked around them then suddenly he snapped to his cronies, "Come on, we'll finish this later."

With her heart pounding Sinead watched the bullies walk across the playground to the classroom entrance.

"Is Matthew really in hospital?" asked a girl who was in Sinead's class.

Sinead nodded.

"What happened?"

As they walked across the playground Sinead told her and several other girls what had happened. She also handed out some of the Bully Squad's leaflets she was carrying.

Before going into his class Robbie smiled at her. "Thanks Sinead."

Before going into her own class Sinead asked her teacher for permission to put up the poster.

****

That morning, Jane and Patrick sat in the sitting room. Patrick was sleeping. If Patrick had been well, Jane thought, as she watched him breathing deeply, I wouldn't have let Jack go to school. She sighed heavily. Patrick's getting worse. She wondered did her children notice. They must do, she thought sniffing. They're probably too frightened to say anything. She thought now about Patrick's assessment this afternoon. She knew he was much worse and it would depress him to hear it from the doctor. She rose and with a glance at Patrick slipped out to the kitchen.

14

The following month, with the website up and running and their email address set up, Nora and Jack began to read some of the emails that children had sent.

After another interview with Maudie's, Uncle Freddy, who wrote almost a whole page on what Jack and the Bully Squad were doing, other schools had been encouraged by their teachers to contact them. Over twenty schools had now joined in the bully campaign.

****

Two bigger boys are hitting me every day. They always stop me on the way home from school. I'm really frightened. Please....please help me. Tommy Curran. I am at, The Waterside Primary school.

My form teacher, Mr. Johnston always slaps me on the back of the head. I don't do anything to deserve it. Yesterday he hit me really hard. I keep getting headaches. I don't know what to do. I told my mum, but she doesn't believe he's hitting me for nothing. What can I do to make him stop? Paul Irons.
PS. I'm in St. Patrick's School.

Bully Squad please help me. Some boys are teasing me every day about my height. I'm really big, you see, bigger than everyone at our school. I'd do anything to get them to stop teasing me and making little of me, if you'll pardon the pun. Brian McGuire. Christopher College.

Dear Bully Squad, my little sister and I are being bullied by older girls. It's because we don't have a Daddy. We haven't told Mummy yet because she is always worried about paying bills and things. Please help us. Josephine and Margaret Kelly. Little Hampton School.

Dear Bully Squad, I really need help. Some boys from another school stop me every day on the way home. Last week they stole my watch. I had to tell a lie and tell my Daddy that I lost it. He was angry with me. Vincent Norby. St Columba's school.

Jack frowned when he heard Nora sniffing. He turned to see tears running down her face.
"Nora, what is it?"
"There are so many of them- so many being bullied. Jack, we can't do it all. All the schools have to form a bully Squad…All the schools in the town."
"I guess," said Jack frowning again as he read the email from Paul Irons again. "Paul is in Matthew's school. Let's see if he can sort it." Reaching for his mobile he rang Matthew's number.

Nora listened as Jack explained to Matthew what was happening to Paul.

****

The following morning Sinead walked behind Mr. Johnston as he headed across the playground. She could see little Paul standing with a group of other young boys watching another boy as he balanced on his hands and began walking in a circle around the playground. She focused her mobile camera when she saw Johnston look around then move to the side towards Paul and the other boys.

Suddenly, Johnston slapped Paul hard on the back of his head almost throwing the little boy off his feet.

"Behave yourself, Irons!" he snapped then walked on.

Sinead stood there, too shocked to say anything. Paul too looked shocked. He stood almost in tears rubbing the back of his head. The other boys didn't notice. Flicking her mobile Sinead checked what she had taken on the camera. Seeing it on the mobile only made it look all the more serious. "Bastard," she thought. Her heart was thumping with anger as she hurried to show Matthew.

That morning Matthew and Paul stood outside the Head's office.

Inside they could hear Johnston saying, "That's a lie. I'd never hit a child!"

"Mr. Johnson," said Mrs. Cavanaugh the Head teacher. "You have been hitting this boy on the back of the head, torturing him. He has complained. I must take action. Now gather up your belongings and leave my school immediately."

There was a short silence until Johnston erupted. "It's his word against mine! I'll take it to a tribunal! You'll pay for this!"

"No Mr. Johnston, you'll pay for it. When this gets out, you'll never get work in a school again. Now, PLEASE gather up your belongings and leave my school. IMMEDIATELY!"

Matthew, and Paul, who was trembling, stepped away from the door as the burly form teacher came out. His face was red with anger. He glared at Paul and took a step towards him.

"I wouldn't," said Matthew stepping in front of the frightened boy.

Johnston ground his teeth then with a snort he headed down the corridor to the locker room.

Just then Mrs. Cavanaugh came to the door of her office.

"Matthew, Paul won't you come in."

****

Ten minutes later Matthew joined Sinead in class.

"Sorted," he whispered. "Johnston's leaving."

Sinead smiled.

In the playground at dinnertime Matthew text-ed Jack, to tell him that Johnston had, "got the boot." He went on to say that it was time to try and get all the other schools in the town to set up a Bully Squad in each of them.

"Jack says we should meet," he said to Sinead. "I've suggested, Rocky's Restaurant. It's almost between our two schools."

"When?"

"Sunday. Is that OK with you?"

Sinead smiled. "Anything with you is OK with me," she said.

Matthew looked around then suddenly grabbed her and pulled her to him and kissed her. They grinned at each other when they parted.

****

Around the same time, Megan, Danni and Elizabeth were standing near the playground toilets discussing their money situation.

"I'm into Carlin and Gallagher for forty quid," whined Danni. "They told me they won't let me have any more stuff if I don't pay up. Gallagher says he'll do me over if I don't cough up the money before next week. What are we going to do?"

"We," snapped Megan. "You're the one who owes them. Well I do too, but only a tenner." She looked around the playground. "We need money and there's no use twiddling our thumbs. We daren't tackle any of the brats here." She glared across at Jack and the gang. "If it hadn't been for them…"

"But it was," said Danni. "Megan what are we going to do? I need to get more stuff and also pay off Carlin and Gallagher."

****

Early that evening the three bullies walked into Marks and Spencer on lower High Street. They headed straight for the new dress section. As they were about to pass the perfume counter Danni looked around, then just as they passed it she snatched a small box off the counter and hurried on. When they reached the dress section she slipped the box of perfume into the inside pocket of her denim jacket.

Two minutes later Megan was approaching one of the sales assistants who was standing by the Fitting Room. "Two items to try on," she said.

A minute after, Danni arrived, carrying three dresses. One was hidden under the other two. "Two items to try on," she said. The assistant handed her two small plastic stickers then turned to Elizabeth who was standing with three dresses.

"Three dresses to try on, Miss," said Elizabeth.

Inside Danni reached over the cubicle and handed one of her dresses to Megan. Taking a pair of wire cutters from her bag she quickly cut the security tab on the dress then pulled it on. She grinned as she pulled her jeans and blouse and jacket on over it.

Five minutes later they left the Fitting Room.

As they were passing the perfume counter on the way out Megan snatched a bottle of perfume in a yellow box that said 1818 and slipped it into her jacket.

Giggling and laughing the girls hurried up the High Street.

"That was easy," laughed Megan. "Now let's see if we can sell the perfume and dress and we have some cash for drugs and maybe a little to pay back Gallagher and Carlin."

****

It was around eight o'clock; after Jack and Daisy had checked the bully squad's emails, that Jane told Jack and Daisy that their father was due home some time ago. "He just went down to the Mickey's Paper Shop for a newspaper and some sweets. I reckoned it would take him ten minutes. It's almost half an hour. Jack, would you go and have a look for him?"

"Sure."

"I'll go with you," said Daisy.

As they hurried down the street Jack was thinking about his father. He had grown more vague and quiet. He felt a little guilty that he had been so caught up in spreading the Bully Squad's message that he hadn't been helping out at home. His mother needed him, he knew that.

When they reached Mickey's, Jack and Daisy went inside. "Mickey, did my Daddy come in today?"

Mickey, a short middle-aged man with an absurd comb-over and glasses, frowned.

"Yes, he bought the Daily Mirror and a packet of gums. That was about twenty minutes ago. Why?"

"Oh nothing," said Jack. "Thanks."

Mickey watched them leave. He frowned as he thought about the children's father. Patrick was a regular customer, but he had noticed a sort of vagueness and hesitation when he came into the shop. Sometimes he thought that Patrick didn't really know what he had come in for. The shop owner shrugged. None of my business, he thought.

"Mum he left the shop about twenty minutes ago," said Jack glancing at Daisy as he spoke into his mobile. "Look, Daisy and I'll go on down the street and search around. He might have gone towards the big shopping center. Yes…yes I'll keep you informed every ten minutes. If Daddy comes home you'll let me know? Yes. See you, and Mum, don't worry, we'll find him."

"Come on, Daisy." With his heart pounding, Jack and Daisy ran down the street.

They found their father standing at the junction of the Strand Road and the road that led to their street. He was looking puzzled. When he saw them his face broke into a smile.

"You OK, Daddy?" asked Jack studying him.

"OK? Yes, I was just on the way home. What are you two doing here?"

"We were looking…" began Daisy, but Jack nudged her sharply with his elbow.

"Mummy has supper ready," said Jack, giving Daisy a warning look.

"Right, let's go. We don't want to keep your Mum waiting," said his father beginning to walk in the other direction.

"Daddy," exclaimed Jack, "this way."

His father turned. He smiled. "Oh yes."

As they walked up the road Jack was worried. Did daddy not know the way home? He's getting worse, he thought.

Later that night he overheard his father talking to his mother in the kitchen.

"Jane, I forgot where I lived…I forgot…"

Slipping back upstairs Jack hurried to his room. His father *had* forgotten the way home. He sniffed then suddenly buried his head in his pillow.

15

On Sunday afternoon, Megan and the others joined the crowds of shoppers walking into Marks and Spencer. The store was packed.

"Now you know what we have to do?" whispered Megan. She glared at Elizabeth. "Stick to the plan, you suss out the perfume department. When the assistant is showing you some of the more expensive stuff, we'll come over. Leave it to us then. But just keep the assistant busy…"

Ten minutes later, with a hand-bag full of boxes of perfume Megan and Danni were pushing through the shoppers heading for the door. A few meters behind them Elisabeth was hurrying to catch up.

Suddenly she was pushed aside as two security guards, a burly woman and a bald-headed man pushed past her.

Elizabeth stopped, her eyes widening as she saw the woman speak into a small microphone on her uniform. Elizabeth looked to her right and another security guard appeared.

Megan and Danni, walking quickly, left by the front entrance that would take them onto the main street. There, they slowed down and waited for Elisabeth. It was then the woman security guard grabbed Megan by the arm.

"Excuse me, miss, but I have reason to believe you have taken some items from our store that you haven't paid for."

Megan tried to break the woman's grip.

"Let me go."

Danni was just making up her mind to run when another woman security guard and a man appeared.

Elizabeth, with her heart pounding, watched as Megan and Danni were forced back into the store. Then with her heart beat racing with fear she hurried away.

****

Around the same time, in Rocky's Café, the Bully Squadders were all gathered around a wide round table sitting at the front window.

After they had all ordered coffee Jack said, "What we need to do first is write a letter to each of the schools telling each Head about our Bully Squad and website. If they agree with our objectives we can then get some posters and leaflets printed up."

"That's a great idea, Jack," said Matthew.

"I have a list of all the schools in the town," said Tommy. "I got the addresses out of Yellow Pages."

Jack smiled at his pal. Tommy had changed this past month from the silly joke cracker and not too serious teenager, to someone he knew would always be his friend.

"You know, what we really need to promote our website and email number is to get on TV, or radio," said Sinead shortly after the waitress had arrived with their coffees.

"TV? How are we going to do that?" exclaimed Catherine.

"What about your Uncle Freddy, Maudie?" asked Nora. "Do you think he would have any connections that way?"

"Dunno. I could ask him, but I don't think so. My uncle just does his column part time. He's sort of semi-retired really. His editor only allowed him the write up he gave us because he too was bullied when he was at school," said Maudie.

As they were talking Jack was thinking about TV and radio. The only way to get the television companies interested was if they had a…

"A march!" he exclaimed, suddenly smiling.

"What?" asked Matthew.

"If we could organize a march… through the town, down Main Street," said Jack almost on his feet with excitement.

"A march?" exclaimed Sinead frowning. "With who?"

"Everyone," answered Jack.

"Everyone? You mean…adults as well?" said Tommy.

"Sure, everyone, anyone, adults are being bullied as well," said Jack. "I've been doing a lot of research on the internet. Many adults were bullied when they were young. Some of them haven't got over the…tra…trauma of being bullied. We have to get a march organized. It's the only way to advertise our bullying campaign."

"Jack, maybe we should wait until we see what answers we get back from the rest of the schools," said Matthew. "If we get enough then maybe we can get word to all the schools about a march. Hopefully many of the parents of the pupils will march with us. A march is a brilliant idea, but it will take a lot of organization."

Jack looked around the table. Everyone was nodding their heads.

"Right, it's agreed then," he said. "We wait and see what response we get from our letters and then make a decision from that, OK?"

Everyone nodded.

****

"Did you hear about Megan and Danni?" said Tommy at break time on Monday morning.

"Yes," said Maudie. "Caught filching in Marks and Sparks yesterday."

"Stupid cows," exclaimed Catherine. She smiled. "They deserve it."

Nora frowned. "No they don't, Catherine. They were just in a bad situation. They needed money, so they had to steal it. They needed drugs. It was taking drugs that caused everything that happened to them."

****

It was over a week later before the answers to ninety percent of the letters the Bully Squad had sent out began to filter to Jack's house.

Over ninety-five percent of the letters were positive.

****

Meanwhile Jack's father had grown much worse, so weak that he was hardly able to hold a cup and was finding it impossible to use a spoon or knife and fork.

In the evening, before he went out to see Nora, Jack would sit with his parents in the sitting room, sometimes looking over at his father who would usually be asleep. All the fun seemed to have drained from Patrick and he sat, sometimes for hours, just staring at the TV. Jack's mother now looked totally exhausted and had dark rings around her eyes.

Later, Daisy and Jack pretended not to look as their mother lead Patrick by the hand out to the toilet. Daisy sighed and there were tears in her eyes. Jack frowned and went over to her.

"Come on, Daisy, let's check our emails," he said quietly.

****

It was on one of those evenings, when his father was awake and they were watching TV that the phone call from the local radio station came.

Out in the hall Jack took it. One of the more popular local radio news reporters had heard about Jack and his bully campaign and was interested in doing a short interview on the radio. At first Jack wasn't sure and believed he would be too nervous to do the interview, but then he thought, it would be a great way to let people know about the march…that he hadn't organized yet. So it was agreed he would come for the interview on Friday after school. The interviewer said it was OK to bring some of his friends.

When he told his mother, she didn't show much enthusiasm for it and Jack could understand why. But Daisy was delighted. She knew if Jack was interviewed on the radio and knowing how enthusiastic he was about The Bully Squad, more and more people would hear about their bully campaign.

The following morning Jack told the others about the forthcoming interview. He had also text-ed Matthew who promised to turn up at the Radio Station as well.

****

Five of them sat opposite Joey McTavish the middle-aged Scot who was to interview them.

McTavish was a young man with bright orange hair and a tuft of hair growing on the front of his chin beneath his lower lip. His eyes were darting and to Jack he seemed as if he was plugged into an electric socket.

Matthew, Jack, Nora, Tommy and Daisy glanced at each other nervously as the interviewer introduced them.

"How did the Bully Squad begin?" he asked.

Jack, who was to be the spokesperson for the group began, telling McTavish how his little sister, Daisy, was being bullied and how he didn't know or suspect it. Jack then went on to talk about Nora and how she had helped his sister.

Twenty minutes later the interviewer asked, "And you're having a march? Who do you want to go on this march?"

"All children who are being bullied," answered Jack. "All parents of the children who are being bullied, all parents who have been bullied themselves, every pupil from every school in the town. In fact, everyone who is sympathetic to our cause."

"Whew," exclaimed McTavish, "that's a lot of people. If only a quarter of them turn up it will be some march."

"I don't know how many will turn up, we in the Bully Squad," said Jack smiling at the others, "are hoping for a good crowd. It will be an orderly march through the main part of town, to show everyone we mean business. Any bully will have to watch out. The Bully Squad is in town."

It was then Tommy shouted, "Who ya gonna call?"

Grinning the teenagers answered. "The Bully Squad."

McTavish grinned as well. Now he had a slogan to use.

When the interviewer was finished he said to Jack and the others. "I'll make sure more publicity goes out from the station about the march. Thanks everyone. That was a great interview. Hopefully we'll have you all back again after the march." Then as Jack and the others filed out of the small studio McTavish said into his microphone, "Well, everyone out there, if you're being bullied, who ya gonna Call?"

****

Later that evening as Jack was about to go for a walk with Nora he looked at Daisy who was sitting in the corner watching TV.

Jane and Patrick sat together on the sofa.

"Daisy, I'm heading out to Nora for a walk. Want to come with us?"

Daisy frowned. "No...I'd only be in the way." She glanced at her mother. She didn't seem to have heard.

"Daisy, come on," said Jack. "Come on."

Smiling Daisy rose. "Would it be OK, Mummy?" she asked.

"OK?" Jane frowned at her.

"To go out with Jack and Nora?"

"Jack and…Nora? Oh, sure, luv. Don't stay out too late."

Quickly Daisy slipped past her and in the hall they put on their coats.

"Jack, are you sure you want me to come? Nora mightn't…"

"Daisy, I'll always want you around me," said Jack smiling. "I'm still very sorry for not being there for you when you were being bullied."

Daisy looked up at him, tears bubbling in her eyes.

When she heard the front door slam Jane sighed.

****

That night when he returned, Jack checked the emails, forwarding some to the other Bully Squads in other schools. It was when he read the last one that he almost cried aloud. That night he hardly slept.

16

"We have to have an urgent meeting," he said to the others that morning at school. "I've already text-ed Matt and Sinead."

Nora studied his serious face. She knew something was wrong. "Jack, what is it? What's wrong? Is it about the march? What?" asked Nora.

Jack looked around the others. "I just can't tell you, not until we have the meeting. Are you all OK for Rocky's after school?"

"I can't make it," said Maudie. "I have to be home early. Mums going to some sort of anniversary do with her boyfriend. She asked me to be home from school as soon as I can to baby-sit our wee Paul."

Jack looked around the others. "What about the rest of you?"

"Jack, why can't you tell us what it is?" said Tommy.

"Tommy, I..." began Jack gulping. "Please, just wait until the meeting, I'll tell everyone then. Are you coming?"

"Of course," said Tommy. He frowned as they all walked into school. Whatever it was it had to be bad for Jack not to tell him. Christ, he thought, what is it?

He glared at Elisabeth who was just passing. Her head was bowed as she walked through the door into class.

****

Matthew and Sinead and another girlfriend of Sinead's, a tall, gangly girl called, Francis, were already there when Jack, Nora, Tommy, Catherine and Daisy came into Rocky's. They all ordered coffee, except Daisy who ordered tea.

Jack licked his lips after a sip of Latte then took a deep breath. As he did he glanced at Nora. "I got an email last night and I don't know what to do about it. It doesn't fit into bullying, but at the same time it does."

Nora frowned. Jack had told her earlier what was in the email. She was still shocked. She listened when Jack read out the text of the email.

For several seconds no one spoke. Catherine was the first. She was almost in tears. "We have to help her," she said hoarsely.

"Of course we have to," said Matthew. "But how? What do we do? I don't think we should trust the Social Services with this. Remember how they handled that case with the little girl who was badly beaten and died."

Tommy was angry as he exclaimed, "We should beat the bastard to death!"

Jack stared at him. That was how he felt, but they couldn't. But how were they going to help the little girl. She hadn't told them where she lived. He hadn't answered her email in case…

Catherine had been tearful all through the conversation, but her words shocked the others. "I was abused by our neighbor next door. My Mummy didn't believe me at first, but my Daddy did. It was an awful time. I was afraid. I know the little girl must be terrified. She said her uncle will kill her if she tells. That's what our neighbor said to me. And you know," she added, tears filling her eyes, "I felt so bad, so dirty…I…" and suddenly she was crying.

Tommy rose and went to her putting his arms around her. "Catherine, don't cry. That's all in the past now…"

"Is it, I still feel awful. I can't get it out of my head. Sometimes I wake at night and can't get to sleep thinking about it." She trembled.

It was Nora who spoke next and she knew Jack would be angry with her. "Jack, *we* are the Bully Squad. This little girl's problem is not ours. This is for the Samaritans or Save the Children or some other organization, not us."

Jack's eyes widened as he glared at her. "What? Nora, you're not saying we should forget about it." He studied her. Of all the Bully Squad members, Nora was the one he admired the most. He had grown to like her so much.

"No, I'm not saying that…" began Nora.

"Then what are you saying?" snapped Jack, suddenly angry.

"Jack, I'm just saying, it's not a bullying issue. Bullying is a problem we can help with. This is different. We don't have the experience for the little girl's problem."

Jack looked around the others. Some of them were nodding.

"Why couldn't we pass on the information to the Social?" said Francis quietly. "I know they made a mess of that little girl's problem a year ago, but surely they wouldn't make the same mistakes?" She looked around. "Would they?"

There was silence for several seconds as each of the Bully Squad took a sip of coffee. Jack was the first to speak.

"I can't forget about it. I can't let it go," he said, glancing at Nora. "If you're all not in, then I'll do it myself."

"Do it?" exclaimed Tommy. "Do what?

Jack looked at his pal. "I'm going to contact her and find out where she lives. Then I'm going to go around to her house and tell her parents."

"No," gasped Nora.

"Jack!" exclaimed Daisy.

It was then Jack rose to his feet. "That's it, the meeting's over." He glared at Nora.

Just then Matthew rose to his feet. "Jack wait, sit down. Let's talk about this. There has to be a better way."

"There has to be, but I don't know what it is, Matt," said Jack, still on his feet.

"Jack," said Nora quietly, "Sit down. Let's talk over what we should do…"

"But you don't want to do anything!" snapped Jack, his eyes blazing.

"I didn't say that, I just said, it wasn't in our experience to help the little girl. If you barge around to her house she might be so frightened she would deny everything. She's frightened now. She is afraid to tell her parents. Do you think she would be glad you did? It would be your word against her uncle's."

Jack slowly sat down. Nora made sense. They would have to have a better plan. But he knew they had to help the little girl.

"I think you should try and find out her name and where she lives," said Sinead.

Everyone looked at her.

"We have to find out everything about her. How do we know she's telling the truth?" said Sinead, glancing at Matthew.

"Who would lie about something like that?" exclaimed Catherine.

"There are people who would tell lies just to get attention," said Nora. "We've all come across them."

"Then what are we going to do?" snapped Jack, growing angry with Nora again. "Look, are you all in? Are you going to help? If you are then let's get a plan sorted out."

For the next half hour everyone offered suggestions on what to do, but they all agreed that Jack should answer the little girl's email, find out her name first and if possible find out where she lived and what school she attended.

****

That night Jack's father collapsed. They had been sitting in the kitchen having supper when suddenly he rose to his feet. He was trembling all over. With a cry he stumbled to one side, his hand sliding along the table. He fell onto the hard tiled floor. Blood was pumping from his head as Jack phoned the ambulance.

17

It was after two in the morning when Daisy, Jack and their mother returned home. Patrick would have to stay in hospital for a few days.

Downstairs Jane sat sipping a cup of tea. "Looks like a stroke," she thought, as she remembered the doctor's words. "Oh God help us."

****

Upstairs Jack checked to see if Daisy was sleeping. When he went into her bedroom he could hear her crying.

"Daisy," he whispered, sitting on the bed and stroking her back. "Daddy will be OK. Don't worry."

"No Jack," sniffed his sister. "He won't be OK. I know it. So don't pretend to me. I'm not stupid…"

"I'm sorry. But maybe in hospital they'll find out something…be able to help him…" He stopped, as tears ran down his face.

Daisy looked at him and suddenly they were crying and hugging each other.

When he left Daisy twenty minutes later she was almost asleep. As he pulled on his pajamas he remembered the little girl. He couldn't let her down. Going into the computer room he booted up the computer and was soon contacting the little girl's emails.

In the morning he checked, but there was no reply.

"Do you need us to go with you to the hospital, mum?" he asked later.

"No, no, I'll be fine," said Jane smiling. "You two get to school. And don't worry. Daddy will soon be home."

Later as she watched her two children head down the street to school she said a silent prayer that everything would be all right.

****

That morning Jack told the others about his father collapsing. He also told them he had replied to the little girl's email, but hadn't had an answer yet.

"Did you hear about Megan's old man?" said Tommy, looking across at Elisabeth who stood alone near the toilets.

"No, what happened?" asked Catherine.

"He shot Joe Carlin in the legs."

"What?" exclaimed Nora, Jack and the others.

"Yes, it was on the news this morning. Megan is to be charged with theft and when her dad found why she was stealing, he sought out Carlin and plugged him. Apparently Megan's dad's been in prison before."

"Megan's dad?" exclaimed Catherine. "Really, he shot Carlin?"

"Yes."

"Is he OK?" asked Jack.

"Who? Carlin? I think so. He's not dead anyway."

****

When Jack and Daisy came home, their mother told them that Patrick had had a minor stroke. He would be in hospital for the next week or so. They were to go around to see him at visiting time that evening.

****

Later after doing his homework Jack hurried to the computer room and turned on the computer.

He scrolled down the other emails searching for an answer from the little girl. And there it was.

"Katie," he whispered. "Her name is, Katie, and she lives at Nine Coulder Lane. Blessington School." He read Katie's plea.

Please don't do anything. My uncle will hurt you. He said if I told anyone he would kill me. I'm so afraid.

Nine Coulder Lane, he text-ed to Matthew. Then added, *Matt, I'm going to go around there tonight after I come back from the hospital. Do u and Sinead want to come with me? I'll understand if u don't, but I have to do this.*

He received Matthew's text. I've spoken to Sinead. Yes, we're in. But Jack, will they believe us?

They'd better, yes I think they will...I hope they do anyway. I'll meet u around nine-thirty outside Rocky's, OK.

OK, came Matt's reply. *I hope your Daddy's OK. C u.*

****

As they left the hospital around eight-fifteen Jane and the children felt stunned. Patrick could hardly speak. One side of his face seemed to be frozen and his words were slurred.

Earlier Jane had spoken to the doctor.

"If he didn't have Dementia he could get through this, Mrs. O'Hara. We'll keep him comfortable here for the next four or five days. Then I'll be able to give you a good prognosis." The doctor had been encouraging, but Jane felt he was putting off the obvious. Patrick would be wheelchair bound from now on.

On the way home she tried to be upbeat with her children, but she knew by how quiet they were, that they knew their Daddy was worse.

****

Around nine, Jack hurried downstairs. "Mum, I'm off to see Nora for a half an hour or so. Is that OK?" He glanced at Daisy as she rose to her feet to go with him.

"Don't be long," said his mother.

Out in the hall Jack whispered to his sister as she reached for her coat. "Daisy I don't want you to go with me tonight."

Daisy frowned.

"I have to see Nora on my own."

Suddenly angry, Daisy snapped, "Always wanting me to go with you, didn't last long, did it?"

"Daisy I..." began Jack.

"Oh forget it," snapped Daisy. "Just forget it!"

As he hurried down the street Jack thought about how angry his sister was. But he couldn't take her with him, not for this. He knew he would apologize when he got home and hope she understood. He had lied about going to see Nora. It was Catherine who was coming with him, Catherine, Sinead and Matt. He thought now about what he was going to say to Katie's parents. Would they believe him? Oh God, he thought. Would they?

18

Catherine was already on her way to see him and when they met near Strand Road they both hurried to the bus stop.

As the bus carried them into town, Catherine inquired about how his father was. After he told her, Jack showed her the map he had Googled earlier searching for Coulder Lane.

"Nine, Coulder Lane," exclaimed Catherine looking at the map. "It's not that far from Rocky's."

****

When they got to Rocky's, Matthew and Sinead were standing outside. They both looked apprehensive.

"Let's have a coffee first," said Matthew. "We can discuss how we're going to approach this."

"How's the ankle?" asked Jack as they walked inside.

"As good as new, I'm playing five-a-side football at the Gym tomorrow. Guess who's on the opposing team?"

"Smith," grinned Jack. "You'd better watch out."

Matthew grinned. "Yeah, well we'll see."

Inside, after their coffees were served they all drank in silence.

"Could we get in trouble for this?" asked Sinead, breaking the silence.

"I was thinking that," said Catherine. She looked at Jack. "It could jeopardize the Bully Squad, Jack. It could jeopardize the march."

Jack frowned. He thought about it, but then said, "If we can help Katie, then I don't see how. It's just how I'm going to go about it…"

"How *we're* going to go about it," corrected Matthew.

Jack nodded then said, "We can't just knock on the door and say, Mr. and Mrs…" He stopped. "Oh Christ, I didn't ask Katie's second name…"

"She probably wouldn't have given it to you," said Sinead.

Jack nodded. "As I was saying, we can't just knock on the door and say, we know your daughter is being sexually abused by her uncle. Can we?"

The others looked at each other then Catherine said, "Why not? Look Jack, we have to tell her parents. It's the only way to help Katie. That wee girl is probably going nuts with fear. No matter what way we go about it, her parents have to know. If they don't believe us, and somehow I don't think they'll dismiss us out of hand, I can tell them about how I'd gone through abuse." Catherine looked around. There were tears in her eyes.

Jack studied Catherine for several seconds then rising he said, "Right, let's do it."

****

They reached Coulder Lane about twenty minutes later. A car was sitting in the driveway and a light was on in the hall of number nine. Jack took a deep breath. "Come on," he whispered walking to the door.

With great apprehension, Catherine, Matthew and Sinead followed him.

Before ringing the tiny lighted bell, Jack glanced at everyone then pressed hard.

A woman in her thirties, who had long fair hair and a pale complexion, opened the door. She stared at the four teenagers.

"Yes? Can I help you?" she said quietly.

There had been several burglaries in the area a month ago and she regarded the teenagers with suspicion.

"It's about your daughter, Mrs… er…" began Jack.

"My daughter? Which one. I have three." Katie's mother frowned. "What is this?" Turning she called, "Gerry, would you come here, please!" There was a tremor in her voice and Matthew sensed she was afraid. Not good, he thought.

"Katie," said Jack. "You have a daughter called, Katie."

The woman stared at him. "Yes." She turned to look into the hall. "Gerry!" she called again, almost screaming.

Just then, a tall, broad shouldered man appeared. He frowned as he studied the four teenagers.

"What's wrong, Kath?"

"We need to speak to you about your daughter," said Sinead moving closer to Jack. "To Katie."

"Katie?" exclaimed the man. "What about her? You wish to speak with her?" He frowned as he looked at his wife.

Jack looked at the others. "Sir, if we could come in."

"In?" Gerry looked past them. He studied the four teenagers more closely. "Look, what's this about?" he asked, anger in his voice. "If this is some sort of scam…"

"It's no scam, sir," said Catherine. "It's about, Katie. We believe she's being abused."

It was as if Catherine and the others had hit Katie's parents with a huge boulder. The woman cried out and the man backed a step away from them.

"Look, if this is…I'll call the police," he snapped.

"What is this about our Katie?" asked Kath, a tremor in her voice. She turned to her husband. "Gerry, let them in, please."

Gerry quickly made up his mind. "Right, inside, and I should warn you if you try anything, violence, I'm pretty handy with my fists and I won't have any compunction about thumping any of you."

Katie's mother stood aside and Catherine walked past her, followed by Jack, Sinead and Matthew.

Katie's parents looked at each other then followed them inside.

Katie's mother showed them into the sitting room. Two girls, one about nine and the other about seven were sitting on the floor doing a jig-saw.

Jack stared at them. Which one of the little girls was Katie? He frowned. They didn't look old enough to be able to email or use a computer. He looked at Matthew. Matthew looked back. Jack knew he was thinking the same. Was the email a hoax?

"Now what is this about?" snapped Katie's father.

"You said you had three daughters, Mrs. er…"

"Copeland. Yes, what about it?"

"Where's Katie?" asked Jack.

"She's upstairs on her computer…Bebo…I think. Why?"

"Could you get her?" said Catherine quietly. Her heart was pounding. She remembered the time her parents had been shocked. She remembered how afraid she had been.

Mrs. Copeland frowned then turned to her husband. "Gerry…"

Mr. Copeland stared at the teenagers then hurried upstairs.

"You said something about Katie being…" said Kath. She swallowed, unable to say the word.

"Yes. We have a website set up to help children who are being bullied…" began Jack.

"Bullied," exclaimed Mrs. Copeland.

The teenagers heard the relief in her voice.

"A website," said Jack. "Katie contacted me on it just two nights ago. She told me her uncle had been touching…"

Just then Mr. Copeland returned. With him was a pale faced dark haired little girl.

Katie stared at the four teenagers. She gulped.

"Katie," said her mother quietly. "Did you email these…the bully website two nights ago?"

"Bully website? No," exclaimed Katie.

Jack glanced at Matthew.

"Bully website," exclaimed Mr. Copeland. He looked at Kath. "Is our Katie being bullied?"

"Mrs. Copeland," said Catherine. "I know how frightened Katie is. I know, because I too was abused."

Katie stared at her.

"But I thought you said it was a bully website…" exclaimed Kath moving closer to her oldest daughter.

"Yes, it is, but Katie contacted it and told us she was being abused by her uncle," said Jack.

"Katie," said her mother turning to the little girl. "Now tell me the truth. I won't be angry. Did you contact the bully website? Did you say anything about being abused?"

"No, Mummy, I didn't!" cried the girl.

Gerry glared at the teenagers. "What the hell were you thinking about? You've come around to our home and accused…"

"We didn't accuse anyone, Mr. Copeland," said Matthew. "Your daughter, Katie contacted our website. She is being abused, no matter what she says. She's terrified. Look at her."

Frowning Katie's parents studied their daughter.

"Mummy, Daddy, I didn't," cried Katie burying her face in her mother's lap.

With tears in her eyes, Mrs. Copeland turned to Jack and the others. "Please go. If your plan was to upset my family you have succeeded…"

"Mrs. Copeland, we had no plan," said Catherine. "I know Katie is lying. I know, because I lied when I was being abused, but it all came out anyway."

"Proof," snapped Gerry. "Have you any proof Katie emailed your website?"

Everyone looked at Jack as he reached into his Jacket and took out two pages of emails. "It's the one near the bottom," he said quietly, handing it to Gerry.

Katie's father read the emails. His hands were shaking as he handed them to Kath. She read them then suddenly began to cry. "Katie…Oh Katie!"

And suddenly Katie was crying louder. "It was Uncle Stephen…Uncle Stephen. He said he would kill me if I too…told. He said he would kil…."

****

On the way home in the bus Jack and Catherine discussed all that had happened.

"Jack, we'll have to stress on our website that is strictly for bullying. We'll also have to put in the phone numbers, website and email addresses about sexual abuse as well."

That night Jack slipped into Daisy's bedroom.

"Daisy," he whispered.

He knew she was awake. "Daisy…"

"Go away," snapped his sister.

"We went round to Katie's house tonight," whispered Jack. "I'm sorry for not taking you. Matt, Sinead and Catherine came with me. We were able to convince Katie's parents about her uncle."

Daisy sat up. She stared up at his pale face. "You went round…"

Jack nodded.

"Is everything OK, I mean with Katie?"

"Yes, I think everything will be fine now," said Jack. He yawned. "I'd better get to bed. I'm beat."

As he turned to go to the bedroom door Daisy whispered, "Jack, I'm so proud of you."

Jack sniffed, and a tear found its way to his left eye. Then he gently closed Daisy's door and hurried to his bedroom.

19

That morning Megan returned to school. The Bully Squad found out that Danni and her mother had moved away. Megan's father was still in Prison.

It was obvious that Elisabeth didn't want to be friends with Megan and both girls stood at opposite ends of the playground lost in their own thoughts.

But Megan and Elisabeth were not in the minds of the Bully Squad. Everyone was discussing what happened at Katie's house.

And Nora was angry.

"You went round there last night and you didn't ask if we wanted to go," said Nora.

"I just thought you would have been against it," said Jack, a little taken aback by Nora's attitude. "It worked out OK anyway…"

"I didn't say I was against it, Jack," snapped Nora. "I just said that wasn't our remit. Sexual abuse should be reported, but not on our bully website."

"We were talking about that last night. We'll have to add, The Save the Children and Child-line's email and phone number to our site," said Catherine.

"Nora, it all worked out OK. What are you angry about?" said Jack reaching to put his arm around Nora.

With a gruff snort the big girl pulled away, saying, "The Bully Squad isn't just you, you know. It's all of us."

Now Jack grew angry. "What, are you saying we should all have gone around to Katie's house last night? That's stupid!"

"I'm not saying that, but you shouldn't have taken it on yourself to do what you did. That's all I'm saying," snapped Nora glaring at Jack.

"It worked out OK in the end, didn't it? Well didn't it?" shouted Jack.

"Yes it did, but that's not the point," said Nora breathing hard. She was still angry.

"Well what is the point?" shouted Jack.

"The point is, and I'll say it again," shouted Nora. "The Bully Squad is all of us, not just you. You shouldn't have gone around to Katie's house without all of us agreeing."

Jack glared at Nora. He knew she was right, but he was still angry. He was about to say something when Nora turned and walked away.

Everyone stared after her.

****

Around the same time Matthew was lining up with his other four team mates in the school gymnasium. He studied Smith and Simpson who were lined up on the other side.

Mr. Gregory, the PT assistant, with his bright whistle dangling from his neck, held the ball in one hand. He smiled as he studied Matthew. He had been worried that his best player wouldn't be up to scratch for the important schools competition the following Saturday. Five-a-side was fast football and would test all of the boy's stamina.

"Ready?" he said, then suddenly dropped the ball between the teams.

Immediately Joe Moore the outside left on Matthew's team hooked the ball towards him then began to dart to the edge of the Gym. He looked for

Matthew who was running forward then with a quick kick he sent the ball low into the middle.

Instantly Matthew stopped it, turned around and passed it to Eamon Cartin, the outside right, who raced forward down the right hand side of the Gymnasium.

As he did, Matthew moved closer to the opposing side's net. As the ball came over he moved forward getting ready to kick it hard. Suddenly Smith rammed into him sending him flying along the smooth wooden floor.

The PT assistant almost choked with anger as he blew the whistle.

"Foul!" he exclaimed glaring at Smith.

"Sorry sir," said Smith turning and raising his eyebrows to Simpson.

As Matthew scrambled to his feet Mr. Gregory asked, "You OK, Carson?"

Matthew glared at Smith. "Yes sir."

"Good," said Gregory pointing to the penalty spot. "Penalty."

"Aw sir," protested Smith. "It was an accident."

"I don't think so," snorted Mr. Gregory. "The way you tackled Carson, you might have done him an injury. Now watch it."

"You take the penalty, Matt," said Joe.

The ball shot into the net. Matthew's team cheered. Smith scowled.

The game continued for another ten minutes and once again Smith came in with a late tackle bringing Matthew heavily to the floor on his shoulder. Immediately he was on his feet and reaching for Smith.

"Here, here!" shouted Mr. Gregory. "None of that!" He glared at Smith. "Another tackle like that, Smith and you're out of the team on Saturday."

"Sir, it was a fair tackle. You saw it," protested Smith. At this Simpson laughed. Smith smiled.

"Yes I did, and your version of fair and mines are a lot different, Smith. So watch it. Right, there's ten minutes to go. Score is two each."

The game commenced. With a minute to go before the end of the match Matthew had the ball at his feet. From the corner of his eye he saw Smith and Simpson darting in to take him down. Suddenly he stopped and pulled the ball back. Simpson and Smith, unable to stop their tackle collided into each other and fell tumbling to the floor.

"Goal!" screamed Joe Moore as Matthew put the ball away.

With a screaming curse, Smith scrambled to his feet and launched himself at Matthew. Both teenagers fell to the floor punching and kicking at each other.

With a tremendous effort the burly PT assistant pulled them apart. He knew now there was no love left between the teenagers. He pushed Smith away when the boys were parted. Matthew's face was flushed with anger.

Mr. Gregory studied the pair. "I can see there's only going to be one way to settle this between you. Boxing ring at Dinner-time."

Smith's eyes widened. He stared at Matthew. He was smiling.

****

Almost all of Smith and Matthew's class were in the Gym that dinnertime after word got out about the coming fight.

In the boxing ring, Mr. Gregory stood between the two teenagers. They were both wearing boxing gloves. "Right you two, a fair fight. No eye gouging or head butting."

Almost everyone was cheering for Matthew as he touched gloves to Smith's. He was about to turn away and go back to his corner when Smith swung a punch at him. The punch landed high up on Matthew's head, but the blow was enough to swivel him around and he fell sideways against the ropes.

The PT Assistant glared at the grinning Smith as he pranced about the ring, then suddenly Smith turned and was into Matthew punching hard at his already bruised ribs. Gasping with the pain, Matthew grabbed onto the bigger teenager and held on.

Furious, Smith tried to pull away to punch Matthew, but still dazed he held on.

The bell rang for the end of the first round.

Sinead was in Matthew's corner as he staggered back to sit down.

"You OK Matthew?" she whispered.

"Yes," said Matthew. "He caught me there, but he won't do it again."

The bell rang and instantly Matthew was rushing at Smith. The attack shocked and surprised the bigger teenager and he was forced back against the ropes. A left and right, another left and right and he was hanging there open to Matthew's mercy. It was then Mr. Gregory stepped in.

"Had enough, Smith?" he asked.

"Get out of my way!" shouted Smith then lunged at Matthew. But Mathew saw him coming, ducked and shot a hard blow into Smith's midriff. The air rushed from the bully's mouth and as Matthew's fist smashed into his face he fell back onto the canvas. The fight was over.

Smith never heard the cheering of his classmates as he was carried to the School Nurse's office.

****

Three nights later, Jack received a phone call from Katie's mother thanking him for all he had done. He had been about to go out with his mother and Daisy to the hospital to pick up his father.

****

That night Patrick, in a wheelchair was brought into the house. The small sitting room at the back of the garage had been fixed up with a bed. As Jack helped his mother get his daddy into bed, he smiled and said something in hard to understand words. Jane and Jack frowning looked at each other then smiled and nodded.

Later, when Jack and his mother left the room Patrick began to cry.

20

That Friday morning the rain poured down. The weather forecast was for thunder and lightning and heavy showers.

Jack glanced occasionally through the classroom window. Rain was battering against the panes. He knew there would be no let up in the weather. He was worried the rain would deter many from joining the march. His stomach churned with worry.

All that week McTavish had broadcast on every one of his shows about the march to prevent bullying. At the end of each show he almost shouted, "Who ya gonna call?" On Friday at four o'clock, he urged everyone to attend the march.

The march was to end near the Guildhall Square where a platform had been set up for the mayor to give a short speech and welcome the marchers. It was expected that one of the original members of the Bully Squad was to give a speech as well. Jack had been assigned to do it.

Maudie's uncle had written almost a full page on bullying and the newspaper had advertised the march. Leaflets had been distributed to all the schools and everything had been prepared.

Jack sighed. He looked at Nora. She had not spoken to him all week. He wondered would she attend the march.

****

Around three-thirty, with the rain battering down on them, Jack was helping his mother get his father from the car into his wheelchair. The start of the march would be through the main part of town and using her disabled sticker, Jane had parked near Asda's big store.

As they waited in the rain Jack looked around. Apart from Daisy and his parents, only a few pupils from his school were there.

"But then we're early," he thought. He wondered again would Nora come.

"Jack!" hailed someone from the corner of the road. It was Tommy. Walking on each side of him were Catherine and Maudie. With her was a short stout man.

When they came over, Maudie introduced everyone to her Uncle Freddy.

As they were shaking hands, more pupils from Jack's school began to come over. And still the rain poured down.

****

Around five minutes to four the rain suddenly stopped and the sky began to clear. By then there were over three hundred people ready to begin the march.

"Not a bad, crowd," exclaimed Tommy.

"No," said Jack, though he was disappointed. He had expected more pupils from other schools.

Just then one of three double-Decker buses pulled up and two people ran towards them. It was Matthew and Sinead. He grinned at Jack saying, "Nearly our whole school came, teachers and all."

Jack looked at the other two double-deckers. More pupils from other schools were piling out of them.

"God, there must be near on a thousand," exclaimed Tommy.

"Yes," said Jack quietly. He felt like crying. Even if this was the whole crowd, it had all been worthwhile. But more and more people were arriving.

Away at the back of the crowd someone waved. Jack recognized Mr. and Mrs. Copeland. Standing along with them, in matching raincoats, were their three children. Jack smiled when he saw Katie. He waved and she waved back.

Now he looked at his watch. He nodded to Tommy to begin as they had rehearsed.

"When you're feeling down and things look bad," sang Tommy at the top of his voice. *"Who ya gonna call?"*

"The Bully Squad!" yelled all those around them.

As Jack led the marchers down towards the main street, Tommy sang again.

"If you're being bullied, can't tell your dad! Who ya gonna call?"

"THE BULLY SQUAD!" yelled the crowd.

As Jack led the march of over two thousand, people standing along the footpaths joined in. It was then he saw Nora. She was with her father. She smiled at him and mouthed the word, 'sorry.' As he passed, Nora and her father joined the march.

Everything's complete, he thought. We're all here. He smiled down at Daisy who grinned back.

By the time they reached the Guildhall Square over six thousand people had joined the march. Jack led them, to gather around the platform to be welcomed by the mayor, a tall elegant looking man with a white haired moustache and black hair. It took almost ten minutes for the marchers to get into the wide square, which had last Christmas been packed for the singer, Eoghan Quigg from the X Factor who had switched on the Christmas lights. By then there were almost ten thousand marchers.

One of the Council Stewards, who wore a yellow armband, shouted to Jack.

"O'Hara, come up! The mayor is about to begin his speech!"

Raising his hands, Mayor Finlay waited until some of the clamor had died away. By then Jack was standing beside him. The mayor smiled at Jack and whispered, "It's a success boy. Well done."

"Ladies and gentlemen, boys and girls," he began, "we are here to welcome members of a new fight against bullying, the Bully Squad. As you all know it has been set up by Jack O'Hara and several of his friends to help those who are being bullied, beat the bully. And after this march I believe this town will have been rid of the scourge of bullying. No child, or adult," he added, "will feel alone and cut off because they have the most popular website in our county, www.thebullysquad.co.uk. I know you will all remember it. And now," he said turning to Jack, "I'd like to introduce you all to Jack O'Hara."

"Hurrahhhhhh!" screamed the crowd.

As the crowd cheered, Jane bent to look at Patrick. Tears were running down Jack's father's face and he was smiling.

Grinning awkwardly, Jack took a step to stand in front of the microphone.

"Hello," he said tapping the top of the microphone.

The sound of the sharp clang was drowned out by the cheering crowd.

"First of all I'd like to thank Mayor Finlay for welcoming us and the council of the town for allowing us to have a march."

There was more cheering before Jack could continue. As he did, Mayor Finlay beamed at him.

"When we set up the bully squad all those weeks ago," continued Jack, "Little did we know the extent of bullying there was in our town." He looked at Daisy. "When I found out my little sister was being bullied I couldn't believe it. I was living under the same roof as she was and yet she was too terrified of the bullies to ask me or my parents to help her. And this is how the bully works, through fear, but no more. Now in every classroom there are posters with helpline numbers, child-line numbers, email addresses, websites for any child who is being bullied to seek help. In every school there is a Bully Squad. And the Bully Squad are there for anyone to go directly to them and ask for help. And it will be given, willingly. No child should every fear the bully or bullies."

Jack looked around the crowd. They were all silent listening to his every word, but he had no more to say. It was done. The Bully Squad was a success.

He smiled then shouted, "So who ya gonna call?"

Immediately a resounding, **"The Bully Squad!"** rang around the square.

Smiling Jack held his hand to his ear. "Sorry, I didn't hear what you said. Who ya gonna call!"

This time the answer, **"The Bully Squad!"** was almost deafening.

****

That night, Jack and his family watched the news. Jack grinned when he saw himself standing beside the Mayor. He listened again to his speech. He wished now he had rehearsed one, but he had said it all.

21

EPILOQUE

Jack got out of the taxi and walked slowly towards The Ardlough Home for the disabled and elderly. He sighed as he walked through the door. It would be a while before he could get up to see his father.

As he headed to his father's room he glanced at the news board near the Foyer. Posters of child-line, helpline and Bully Squad information filled it.

His father was sitting in the big room where all the more disabled patients came to every day. The TV in the corner was loud. An old movie was on, a western, and Randolph Scott was facing down a gang of outlaws.

Not one of the patients was watching TV.

Jack stopped beside his father and knelt down. He had a lot to tell him.

He was eighteen, and tomorrow he was going to University. Tommy, Nora, Catherine, Matthew and Sinead were all going to the same University. They had remained friends, growing even closer as they fought to get more grants for child-line and develop the Bully Squad.

Jack spoke to his father slowly, not sure if he understood, or heard anything he was telling him now.

A young male Care Assistant came over as Jack was about to leave. "I have to take your father back to his room for awhile. He needs changed. I won't be long." He smiled.

Jack stood up. "No problem," he said quietly. "I have to be going anyway."

As the Carer was about to wheel Patrick away, Jack's father began to get excited and said something.

"Wait!" Jack said to the Carer. He bent to his father. "What, what is it, Daddy?"

His father really tried hard to say the words. But Jack heard them.

"It...it... was b...b... big, wasn't it?"

"Big? What was big?"

"B...big... P... P... Por..."

It was then Jack understood. "The Porpoise," he exclaimed. "You remembered about the Porpoise." Tears ran down his face as he watched his smiling father being wheeled away.

Then still crying he turned and walked out of the room.

Check out Jack Scoltock's other books
Please leave a review

Made in the USA
Charleston, SC
25 April 2015